SUGARMAN

by

Vincent Vargas
& Geraint Jones

Copyrights

Published independently by Geraint Jones and Vincent Vargas 2019

All standard laws and restrictions apply to any and all sharing or republishing without express written permission of the authors.

About the authors

Geraint Jones deployed as an infantry soldier on three tours of duty to Iraq and Afghanistan. Upon leaving the military, he worked to protect commercial shipping against Somali and Nigerian based piracy. He has co-written bestsellers on both sides of the Atlantic, including two with James Patterson. Geraint has his own series of historical fiction novels with Penguin, and his Afghanistan memoir Brothers In Arms was published this year by Pan Macmillan. Geraint writes full time from his home in Wales.

Vincent "Rocco" Vargas was born and raised in the San Fernando Valley of Los Angeles, California. After several years of college baseball, Vincent enlisted in the US Army and went on to serve three combat deployments with 2nd Battalion of the elite 75th Ranger Regiment. After four dedicated years of active duty service to his country, he joined the U.S. Army Reserves and continued his service. In 2009 he became a Federal Agent with the Department of Homeland Security, and was a Medic with the Special Operations Group.

Dedicated to the men and women of the Border Patrol.

Honor First.

CHAPTER 1

In the beginning, there was no laughter. Instead there was shouting, and screams, and plenty of promises - none of them good. I learned quickly as a boy that violence is not only the answer; It is the question. It is the cause.

It is life.

Violence is life, and life is violence. Little wonder that I became a soldier. No surprise that I went to war. Not much older than a boy I fell in with a generation of warriors who had come to answer a call; maybe their country's, maybe their own.

I didn't think too much about why I was there. Why we were doing what we were doing. Going where we were going. It just seemed a hell of a lot safer than being around my parents. If that sounds stupid to you, then you've never been a punchbag with no one around to watch your back. In Iraq I had enemies, and they were armed, but then so were my big brothers. Growing up no one would speak for me. In the Army, I had people who would kill and die for the angry young kid in their platoon. That changed things for me; I didn't just want someone to watch my back. I wanted to do the same for them.

In time I became one of the big brothers, and in Afghanistan it was me who was leading the way. The big bad door kicker whose only worry was failing my warriors. They would chew bullets for me. Risk everything if I went down and needed dragging out of the fire. If I went down for good, I knew that they would remember me with ink on their skin, and drinks in their hands. I never knew what I wanted from life, but there, with them, I knew what I needed, and I had it;

Brotherhood.

One of those brothers is Ethan. He's sitting across from me now, his head in his hands, sweat creeping through his knuckles. There's a rifle at his feet, another across his lap. The room is hot, and our words have been hotter, but now all is silent. I can't look away from my brother, but for the longest time, I haven't been able to speak. My mouth is as dry as the desert outside, my eyes as wet as the place that we found her.

We've been through hard times, but nothing like this. Still, I remember the words my drill instructor once shouted at me, like he is beside me now, twenty years later, his tobacco breath and spit in my ear; "Ranger up!" He screams at me. "Ranger up!"

I need to Ranger the fuck up.

And so I speak.

"What do you want to do, brother?"

My words come out as a croak, but their intent is as loud as the crack of a rifle.

Ethan's hands come away and his head lifts up. His eyes are red holes in a face pulled tight with pain. I've never seen him like this.

It terrifies me.

"What do you want to do?" I ask again, but I already know the answer.

"Kill them." My brother speaks. "Kill them all."

CHAPTER 2

I'd found her earlier that day. I'd smelled her, not because I'm a fucking hunting dog, but because I know what death smells like. It's more than just what gets into your nose. It's a presence. I've heard my brothers argue over what it is, some saying it's a spirit, others saying it's an evolutionary warning to others, talking about anything from molecules to Jesus. I don't know, and I don't give a shit. I just know that whenever I've smelled it, it's been bad.

On my deployments, it was never the dead enemy that smelled this way on the battlefield. They were fresh kills, still leaking, and they have their own kind of smell. But the rotting ones… The ones that were baked in the sun, they were the innocent. In Iraq, they were truck drivers who'd had their skulls drilled through with power-tools, because they'd taken a delivery to an American base. In Afghanistan, it was a girl who'd dared to go to school. Now, in my home, in my occupation, and on the border, it was the smell of people who died trying to find a new life, or who were caught up in their old one.

We found them in rivers. We found them in deserts. We found them in car trunks, and dry-boarded walls. We found them everywhere. The whole border had a stink, and I'd walked through it with my nose-pinched. You can't breathe it in. Not because your stomach will wretch, but because your heart will bleed. You know how I got through Iraq? I asked my boys if Al-Qaeda had a power tools catalogue, like the ones that came in my mail back home. You know how I got past the dead girl in Afghanistan? I joked that if I didn't have girls distracting me when I was back in school, maybe I wouldn't have ended up carrying an M4 around the fucking desert.

Joke. Laugh. Repeat. That's your SOP, soldier. Wear your kevlar for the outside of your head, and the smile for the inside. Don't like it? Fuck you. Then you've never known war.

And I know war. I know loss. I know death, but…

But this? Feeling the stench of rotting death hit you like a hammer? I can't tell you how I knew it was her and not one of so many others, *but I knew.*

Even though it's pointless I want to run, but my legs aren't listening, my boots dragging to a halt in the red Texan dust. It's been a hundred yards from my truck, but it feels like I just humped a

100k with a ruck. My knees feel hollow. The heat of the south is blazing but I know that's not why stars are coming for my eyes.

I swear, and spit, but my mouth's so dry it just falls pathetically onto my shirt. I'm sinking too fast to give a shit. I know it's her. Know I should call in somebody else.

"You don't need to see this." I say to myself. "You don't *want* to see this."

And I don't. I've never wanted anything less in my life, but she was my friend, and I don't want a stranger to be the one who finds her now. She brought laughter into Ethan's life, and he brought it into mine. I owed her this. Rangers Lead The Way, even in death. *Especially* in death.

I wipe my hands across my face. Sweat and tears come with it. I've never felt so vulnerable. So scared. There's no enemy waiting for me at the bend of that river, only death. I know in my gut that hers is the first of many. Maybe my own.

"I'm sorry." I say as I pick my feet up out of the dirt. "I'm sorry."

I walk on. I lead the way.

And then I see her, and know that nothing will ever be the same.

CHAPTER 3

In life she had been color, and songs, and laughter. In death she was bloated, grey, and silent.

I looked at her for a long time. I didn't run into the water. I didn't fall to my knees. I just looked.

I don't get it. I don't understand. She was so many things to so many people, and now she's just… meat. Decaying meat. Whatever made her *her* has gone. The people that killed her are thieves. They stole her soul. They stole from the world, and everyone that loved her.

I call it in. The trucks take time to arrive. The officers that emerge from the cabs are a mixture of jacked border-bros and older guys with beer and burrito bellies. They know me, don't know her, but my silence is infectious. Usually there would be jokes, and football talk. Today the air feels warm and dangerous like a thunderstorm. No one even speaks to me. They *feel* it. And we've all had those cases. The ones that hit harder than most. They probably think this is some woman that I tried to help with her kids the last time she got picked up crossing. Hard not to get a soft spot for them at times like that. That's what they'll be thinking. Not that I saw this woman as a sister. Not that my best friend saw her as his world. His future. His savior.

I have to tell him.

I turn to look at one of the older agents. One of the guys who was on the job before it became the machine that it is today. These things still shake him, as a human. The younger guys, they're as desensitized to death as the killers who put these people into the water.

He meets my eye. Gives me the nod.

I take one last look to her. They're bringing her naked body out of the water. As I see the cuts and burns in her brown flesh, I'm grateful for the first time that she's no longer with us - her last days would have been agony.

The agents grunt as they lay her grey body in a bag, and pull up the zipper. There is no beauty in death. You go out like yesterday's fucking trash.

There's nothing left for me here.

It's time to break my brother's heart.

CHAPTER 4

Ethan's modest house is outside of town on a small piece of land. He's close enough to his neighbors to yell, far enough for privacy. Real Texas. He flies the state flag beside Old Glory, but there's not a whisper of wind today, and the colors hang as limp as my heart as I step onto the brightly painted boards of his porch.

'Ethan.' I call out. 'It's me.'

No answer. I push open the door.

He's sitting in his chair, a rifle by his feet, another across his lap. He's not looking at me. He's staring out the window.

"I thought about blowing my brains out." Is the first thing he tells me, his eyes still on the desert. "I know she's dead."

He turns. Looks into my face. "And now I know it for sure."

"I'm sorry brother."

His face looks like grey cement. There's no tears, no yelling, just shock, as if this is happening to another person.

"How did I let this happen?"

I sit on the edge of the nearest couch; I don't want my brother to think I'm looking down on him. "Tell me everything from the start." I ask him.

But he doesn't. Not yet. I let him have his silence, and instead I think about the last time I'd come here. It was another world. Ethan's face was red with laughter. Lucia was passing from one room to another like a song. Her son was lying on the floor right there, painting Sugarman masks as Ethan looked on and clapped in pride for each new design. Diego wasn't his son, but he was Lucia's, and he loved them both. The house was full of it. It bounced off the walls. Now, this place was an empty grey cellar. Empty of joy. Empty of hope.

"Ethan. Tell me everything from the start." I said again.

He runs a finger down the barrel of his rifle. He can't look at me. I can feel the guilt and shame coming off him like a fire.

"They took her, Dom. They took her. Now she's dead."

I need to be patient. "Who took her, brother? When?"

"When she went back to see her family."

Lucia was an illegal, and her family were in Juarez. Like thousands of others, she would risk the law to see her blood. This time, she had risked far more. In the last fifteen years, crossing the border had become a game of life and death. I'd seen enough of it to guess what had happened.

"You got a ransom call?"

Ethan slowly nodded his head. Like so many others, Lucia had been held by a cartel who saw a chance of extorting money from their family in the states. If you pay up, they release your loved one…

Sometimes.

"Did you pay it?"

"Of course I fucking paid it!" He snaps. "The first time, and the second time, and the third time! They figured out I was a gringo, goddamnit! They wanted to bleed me dry!"

And I knew Ethan. I knew he would give everything for that woman.

And he had. "I told them that was all I had, Dom!" He pleaded, tears in his eyes now, his hands shaking on the rifle. "I told them that was all I had!"

That was when he had come to me. Told me Lucia was in trouble, no more than that. I hadn't pushed him. I'd been on my way to a call about a body in the river.

I wanted to comfort my brother. I wanted to tell him everything would be alright, but that was horseshit, wasn't it? Things would never be the same, not after this. The woman that he loved had been snatched, treated like a beast for sale, and then butchered. Lucia had brought Ethan back from the edge. Now he was over it without a parachute, and there was no bringing him back.

"Promise me you won't do anything stupid, brother." Was all I could ask him.

"I promised her I would keep her safe." He told me, and I saw tears drop onto his rifle. "I'm done making promises, Dom."

I knew what that meant, and it tore into my heart, but he had earned the right to write his own story.

And so I did nothing but nod, and fight back the lump in my throat that tried to choke off my words. "What about Diego?"

"His birth father, in Juarez. Lucia never talked about him, but I guess… I guess Diego's with him, now."

"And what about me?" I wanted to ask, but didn't. When we were at war, I'd made Ethan promise me that he'd let me bleed out if an IED took my arms and legs. Ethan's body was intact, but his mind was beyond repair. With Lucia gone, he wanted me to honor the same code that I had asked for. He wanted to be left to bleed out.

"I want to be with her, Dom." He told me, reading my thoughts. "I hope you can understand."

"There's another way…"

He shook his head. "I feel like every part of me is on fire, brother. Please. I want this to stop."

No.

I stand.

"I can't let you do it."

He blinks. "*Let* me?"

"So you're on fire. Suck it up. Fight on." The words pour out of me. "You've never been a fucking coward, Ethan, don't start now."

He almost laughs, that fucker. "A coward? You think this is how I wanted to go, Dominic? Hell. You think I'm doing it because of pain? You asshole. Do you even know me? I'm doing this, because if I don't, all this I feel inside right now, this poison, it's just gonna spread. It's gonna get on everyone I meet. Everyone I touch. There ain't no chance of a happy ending for me in this life. I ain't ever getting over this. I'm laying here bleeding out right now, Dom, and you're just too selfish to see it. You know it's done for me."

"You should have come to me sooner!" I shout out. "I could have helped!"

"With what?" Ethan holds up his hands. "With what, brother? We both know what you would have done. We both know that, and I love you for it, but I thought paying them was the best way --"

"She's dead Ethan!" His words have hurt me. "She's dead, brother, and you're gonna just be a fucking coward? You're gonna take the coward's way out, knowing those people that did this to her are still living? Still breathing? And you're okay with that, you fucking coward?"

My chest heaves. My fists clench. I want to hit my brother. I want to hit him, and hold him, because I am fucking terrified. I don't want to live in this world without him, and he knows it…

"How you're feeling right now, brother…" He says, "that's how I felt about her, but a million-fold. You and me, we're brothers. Her and I, we're soulmates. Can you understand me now, Dom? As a brother."

My chin drops to my chest. I want to feel anger.

But I can't.

"I understand, you motherfucker."

I stand in silence then. I know what's coming, for him and me. I just need to ask the question: "What do you want to do, brother?"

My words come out as a croak, but their intent is as loud as the crack of a rifle. Ethan's hands come away and his head lifts up. His eyes are red holes in a face pulled tight with pain. I've never seen him like this.

It terrifies me.

"What do you want to do?" I ask again, but I already know the answer.

"Kill them." My brother speaks. "Kill them all."

CHAPTER 5

Ethan had given me what I wanted - permission to go after the people who had taken Lucia. We both knew this would be the last time that we ever saw each other, at least in this life.

I'd opened my mouth to try and talk him out of it, but my dry lips shut quickly. One look into his eyes was enough. He'd already checked out of this world, and willingly. We were standing on Texan soil. A state had a right to make its own decisions, and so did a man. What happened to Lucia had left him as powerless as a child, but he could still make this call, and it was his to make. I knew the love of brotherhood, but I had never felt anything as strong from my parents, or from a woman. I kept that side of my past in a locker that I didn't ever open, but I knew well enough that I had never experienced the true, beautiful love like the one which had grown between Ethan and Lucia. Like he said, they were soulmates. It was spiritual. Religious. In my own relationships, we'd been more like animals than angels.

My brother had asked me to kill them all and I would carry out his wish, and

I'd do it for the same reason as he was about to take his final action on earth - I couldn't face any other reality. To pretend like this had never happened was no option for me. It would kill me. Drive me to…

"Goodbye, brother."

Time for me to leave. Time for me to step out of one life, and into the next. I'd never been in one place too long. Never had 'family' that lasted more than a few years. God had a plan, and his plan for me was that I lived hard, and lonely. So be it.

"Goodbye, Dominic." He says.

I'm turning my sight away from my brother, but not my back. He knows that this is the greatest love I can show for him. The greatest respect.

I don't look back as I walk down the steps and beneath the flags hanging limp against their poles. I don't look back as I turn on the truck's engine, and pull out onto the dirt.

I never hear the shot, but when my heart begins to thump in my chest, I know that Lucia is no longer alone.

CHAPTER 6

Have you met a soldier at war?

I don't cry for my brother. I don't feel sick. He was there, he was here, and now he's gone. There will come a time - the most horrible moment - where the realization of this will wash through me like acid, but not now. Now I'm at war. I saw him go down, but I have to push on. If I don't, his death will count for nothing. I owe it to him to cut out all emotion. I owe it to him to act like he didn't matter to me. When the work is done, and the war is won, then I can be flesh and blood again. Until then, I'm a soldier.

And a soldier needs intel. That's why I've come into work at the border patrol station. It's not my shift, but this isn't new. There's a lot of guys like me. We don't like time to think, and so we run our engines until we're gassed out. We pick up extra work, patrol extra miles, and shake down whoever we need to so that we don't shake down ourselves. A shark has to keep swimming. We're no different. To stop is to die.

You might think from TV that the agency has walls of LED screens and armies of agents. Nah. This isn't Tom Cruise shit. There's maps on the walls, post-it notes, and stacks of paper-work that will kill more agents through stress and sedentary illnesses than the cartels ever will. There's not many of us. It's not the most attractive job in the world - one bullseye on your head from bad guys, and one on your back from some of your own countrymen - and a tight department budget means tighter wallets. You can live cheap on the border, but even so, the only people in this office are here because they want to be. We each got our own reasons for that - bleeding hearts, to god complexes - but it's as close as a thing I've found to the Rangers since I un-laced my boots for the last time.

I see a group of five or six guys pouring coffee and heading into a briefing room. I take a dirty cup and follow on. The last thing I need is help staying awake, but I'm an intimidating looking fuck - I never once got picked up for a hitch hike - and I worked out years ago that holding some novelty mug with a joke written on it seems to calm people down around me.

The others are taking seats and feel my presence. Some of them were at the river earlier. One of the bros guesses right that I'm here because of that, but not why; "Your girlfriend's tagged, dude. She was cut up pretty bad but damn, nice ass. How long did you wait to call that one in?"

The words mean nothing to me. He doesn't know. He's just sick of death. Scared of it, and trying to hide it. His name is Martin. He's a vet, but he missed out on the shooting wars. I twitch the corner of my mouth enough to soothe his ego.

"What's this?" I ask, using the Hello Kitty mug to point towards a projection screen on the wall.

"Think we got a tunnel." Martin tells me, getting to his feet and handing me a photograph taken from a drone - not the killing kind you see on the news, but one that we picked up at Walmart out of our own pockets. I look it over, but there's not much to see; just an old outbuilding, and a lot of vehicle tracks in the dust.

Martin hands me a second photo. A truck, pulled up outside.

"Got shots of the driver?"

He shakes his head. "We pulled back the drone before they killed the engine. Didn't want to spook them."

One of the lifers from the front of the small room speaks up. Ortega's next up in the chain on command. He's got thirty years on the border, and he wears them heavy. "We're gonna put some surveillance on the ground, Dom. You want the job?"

Ortega knows me, so when I shake my head, it throws him a little. "Jesus," he jokes, "who is she?"

The other agents laugh, but none too loud. I've never been a problem to any of them, but too much happened when I first came here for me to let my guard down. By the time that I was ready for friends, the walls had been built, and so had my reputation - "Dom's a good guy. Solid guy. He's just… he's just a bit of a loner, that's all."

"Where is this?" I ask Ortega.

"I didn't think you wanted it?"

I shrug. "I don't. I just like the puzzle pieces." And that's true. Every little bit of intel counts. You don't go out and find the Mona Lisa. You scratch out thousands of tiles that make a mosaic.

Ortega looks down at a sheet of paper and reads off the location. I pretend to sip my coffee. Pretend to listen to the brief for a few minutes before I quietly make an excuse - "gotta piss" - and slip out of the room.

I don't know what part the tunnel will play in my plans, because I still don't have one. There's something that's been loud in my mind, drowning out even the need for revenge. It comes from being shit on as a kid. Being the runt without a family.

Lucia's son, Diego.

I need to find him.

CHAPTER 7

I don't know much about kids, except that when I was one it wasn't fun, and when I tried to have my own, things got worse.

Diego wasn't like that. He took after his mom, and saw fun in everything. I didn't know much about his dad, but I saw the way he gravitated to Ethan, and I recognized a boy looking for a father figure when I saw one. That's why I need to find him. I'm not slipping into Ethan's shoes, but I want to know that Diego's father will.

I know what actions I need to take, but I don't want to think about the reasons behind it. Thinking has never worked out for me. I need movement. Action.

But the border is a fucking parking lot.

It's worse coming the other way, but still I've got to crawl. I've got time to think, but about what?; Lucia in the river? Ethan saying goodbye?

And so I think about Diego. I think about the smiling kid who'd come out to my ranch so that Ethan could teach him to shoot, like his own dad had done. I enjoyed those days. I took pride in my martial arts, and I took pride in my brother.

Seeing him with Diego and Lucia, I was seeing a man move toward his potential.

My own try at being a dad hadn't worked out so well.

Why would it have? I was twenty-one when I met Rebecca at a bar off base. I was still twenty-one when she told me she was expecting. What else does a young soldier do at that point? He marries the girl he'd met a half dozen times. They get base housing together. Only then, living under the same roof and expecting to bring a human life into the world, do they start to realize how fucked up the other person is; her life hadn't been any better than my own. If she'd have let me see my daughter Mary, when things finally boiled over, I could have forgiven her everything. We'd both been dealt shit hands, but she'd taken her cards, and shoved them down my throat. According to a birth certificate I was a parent. According to my heart I was a father. According to Rebecca I was a danger, and so according to the court I was not a part of Mary's life. I hadn't seen her in 6 years. Didn't know what she looked like, how she thought, what she felt, and what she dreamed of. I assumed, being with her mom that hated me, that she'd feel the same, and I'd had enough shit in my life that I didn't want to drag my dirty feet into hers.

And so I let her be. I kept moving. Patrolled the border. Kept my dick in my pants and my pain in a locker. What was done was done, but there was something I could do for Diego. Make sure he was set. Make sure he had someone in his life who gave a shit. I'd check on his father. Maybe call in now and then. Offer to help with money. Shit, I'd figure it out, but before I did what I'd promised Ethan, I'd carry out this promise to myself. First though, I'd have to find the kid.

All I had to go on was a phone number. It had been in Lucia's belongings, and the paper was old enough that I knew it was someone who mattered to her life, even if they didn't matter to her. I used it to find an address, and I knew enough about Juarez to know that the outlook for this guy wasn't great; I wasn't about to find Diego set up in a Villa, with his schooling covered for life.

If the number and address still held up, Juan Delgardo lived in the Guadalajara Izquierda part of town. It was a front line in the war between the cartels, and clear of the border. I was driving toward it with a familiar lump in my stomach, just like I'd felt when we'd push out on raids in Sadr City. Your brain and body know what's up. Subconsciously, you pick up on threats. You feel the eyes. The look of predators as they assess you, your worth, and the price they'd risk to take it.

I looked at my GPS. I was a couple of minutes from the address, but any hopes I had of Diego's dad being squared away and wealthy were out the window. This barrio was a slum, no other way to describe it. I was passing kids with bare feet, and adults with bare souls, their faces empty as I rolled through the potholes in their streets. I was a stranger, and I had no doubt someone was already putting in calls to let the local *jefe* and *sicarios* know that there was an American on their turf. I should have rented a car instead of using my own truck. Some would say that I can't be too hard on myself for not thinking straight, when the few people that I love in my life have been dropping like flies. But that's exactly my point; if I don't keep my shit together, who's going to stand for them? I just have to hope the local fuckheads are so smashed that they don't think to take pictures of my plates, and that they don't have the connections to run them; yeah, right. The Mexican authorities are riddled with corruption, and in the States, we got a few rotten apples in the basket, too.

"You have arrived at your destination." My phone tells me.

I remember hearing people say that home is where the heart is. My thinking as a kid was 'home is anywhere but here', and I can feel that sense creeping up on me now. I feel dirty being here, like I'm witness to a crime. The crime of giving up, and surrendering to circumstances.

I step out of my truck onto the street. I'm not armed with anything more than a switchblade, since rolling across the border with a firearm was not an option. I feel eyes on me, but I don't see them. I start to step over trash, then give up. The house is decaying, and the yard is a landfill.

I stop at the door. I speak up. "Diego? It's Dom, Ethan's friend."

I hear shuffling inside, but no voices. "Diego?"

More shuffling, then a groan, like a wounded animal is dragging itself through the underbrush. The eyes that I can feel on me are beginning to feel more like crosshairs. No time for niceties. I put my shoulder to the door.

It's time to find this kid.

CHAPTER 8

There's a few things that can get you killed when you enter a room, but the biggest reason is to stay standing like a nice silhouette in that picture frame you just created, and so I move fast and to the right. The only light coming into the building is from behind me, and it's enough for me to catch the source of the shuffling sound, trying to get to his feet.

I grab the zombie by the shoulder and shove it to the ground. I feel another trying to rise from a piss-stinking sofa on the other side of the room. "Stay on your fucking back." I snap in Spanish, and the undead stops struggling.

I don't need to look closely at the man I'm holding to know what I'll see; dried out cheeks. Tight skin. Slack mouth. Vacant eyes. Junkies are the same the world over, and I know that a lot of them got that way because they had lives like mine. That's enough for me to cut them some slack, but not today. I came here for a reason, and I didn't bring my manners. I hit the guy across the face with an open palm; just enough to make his brain open for business.

"Are you Juan Delgardo?" I ask him

three times, each with a bit more force in the words, and my squeeze on his shoulder.

The zombie finally speaks. "*Si.*"

I stand up and haul him up with me. There's just bones to him, as light as an empty tracksuit.

"Where's Diego?" I pull my flashlight and shine it in his red eyes. "Where's you son?"

I see a memory pass over his pass. "Diego?"

"Diego. Your fucking son. Where is he?"

The zombie looks confused. Panicked, even. "I haven't… I haven't seen Diego for months. Not for months."

I shake him. I can hear his fucking bones rattle. I tell him I'll break them one by one to find the truth.

"It is the truth, I promise!"

I don't believe his words, but I believe his eyes. He's gone past the point in life where anything matters except the score. He'd remember seeing Diego because the kid would have helped him get it, or hurt him getting it. Junkies hold grudges, and none more so than against a needy kid.

"If you're lying to me I'll kill you." I growl as I let him go, but Juan Delgardo is already dead, a couple months left in him at most. Then, Diego will be an orphan.

I shake my head. Look around at the zombie's life. Who am I kidding? Diego's already on his own.

I open my mouth to tell him where to contact me if Diego shows up, but I hear noise outside, in the streets; it's breaking glass.

Someone is smashing my truck.

CHAPTER 9

The kids are gone by the time I get outside, but the damage is done. Holes in every window, but the glass was tough, and they didn't get in. I look quickly around the tires, but don't see any flats. At this point it doesn't matter anyway. It's time for me to get the fuck out. I know how these things go. Just like gorillas, humans start with beating chests, and building confidence. First the stones fly, then the bullets.

    I get into the truck, feeling chunks of glass pushing into my jeans. I put her into gear and pull forward, trying to push my upper body and head as far back into the cab as I can. I know I'm not out of this yet, and to prove the point, out the corner of my eye I see a brick come sailing in and bounce off my hood. If I hear a shot, I'll stomp the gas and plough through anything in front of me; my biggest worry now is to find something parked or pulled in front of the narrow streets of the barrio that might block my escape.

    "You fucking idiot!" I shout at myself. I was stupid coming here. What did I expect? To track down a kid in a fucking warzone? That's some Hollywood shit. I've seen enough bodies to know that there are no happy endings, only endings, and I might have just brought mine forward so I could play Brad and Angelina.

"*Fucking idiot!*"

I see a car pulling out of a side street. I step on the gas. If he's trying to block me in I'll T-bone that fucker and drag him back to the border with me. But then I see the shocked look on the man's face, just a guy trying to leave his home, and I shoot by him with a half yard to spare.

I know I'm in trouble. There's no way I can cross the border without explaining the damage to my truck, but the sad truth is that that won't be hard; 'what happened to your car, sir?' He'll ask. I'll shrug and say, '*Mexico.*' And they'll laugh, and I'll laugh, and I'll be back in the states.

But my real problem is before all that. It's the local cops. A lot of them are just cartel guys with a badge. I don't want to deal with them and their questions. They could decide that it's better to be on the safe side, and take me in until they have orders from their bosses. They've got no reason to kill me - not yet - but since when does that matter in Juarez?

I pull out of the barrio and onto a four lane highway. I won't stop, I decide. Keep pushing. Plead shock. Pretend I was in the truck when they smashed it.

I weave in and out of the traffic enough to keep my speed, but not so aggressively that I draw attention; in Central America, that means I can be pretty fucking rough.

I keep looking in my mirrors. No cops. No tails. No reason that there should be, except for the usual; I'm a lone American. A six-foot three-inch dollar sign behind the wheel.

Up ahead I see two local cop cars on the hard shoulder. I breathe a little easier when I see they're already out of the car. I pass at speed, but I can still see the look on the face of the man they've pulled over. He knows he's about to get fucked out of something. Maybe his life.

My heart slows as I see the border ahead. This time of day, it's not at it's worst. Fuck, if I have to, I'll ditch the truck and run. That's why you have insurance, right? I just need to get back to my side of the border. Re-group. Re-think. Shit, I can put on the whole fucking Terminator act, but my best-fucking friend is gone, and so is his soulmate. That stuff is leaking through my armor now. I thought the grief would come at me like a war-hammer, and I could take it on my shield, but this shit is like poison. It's slipping in through the cracks. It's in my nose. My throat. It's starting to choke me.

I need to re-group.

Instead I have to sit in traffic as I'm squeezed toward the border like toothpaste. I look around for danger, but the biggest threats I see in the cars around me are to my humanity; desperate, nervous faces. People fighting their own wars and battles. For good or evil, only God knows. Nothing is simple in life, but death.

Suddenly, I have my realization. I'll come apart if I let myself get sucked into the complexity. The quartermaster of life didn't kit me up to deal with the emotional shit that I face, but he sure as fuck loaded me up when it came to executing in every sense. I'm not a thinker, I'm a do-er, and there's only one thing that I know in my heart needs doing after Lucia. After Ethan.

I hate to think how my face looked as I pulled up to the officers at the border. I had one thought on my mind, and it was ugly. He had to try and speak twice before he got his words out. Probably thought some loco fucking sicario in a smashed up truck was rolling up on them with a death wish. I saw his hand on his hip. Time to smile.

"Good evening, sir." I looked at the damage on my windshield and grinned. "Sure is good to be home."

CHAPTER 10

The border entry wasn't fun. They pulled me in. Asked me a few questions. Made a few calls. The officer that had pulled me in was young, and by the book. Righteous. When they gave me back my keys it was like he was doing me a favor; "Try and be more careful next time."

I wanted to show the little prick that he should take his own advice, and not be a wise-ass when his hands were down by his sides and he was resting his weight on his back foot. But instead of running his nose through his face I thanked him for his service. Arrogant little fuck believed every word and almost bowed back to me.

I wasn't much of a social drinker, but I knew my house was dry, and the bar was next to the liquor store, so what the hell. The place had flags and hunting trophies on the walls, blue-collars at the bar, and silicon and smiles behind it.

"What can I get you hun?" She was half my height, but twice as salty. Young girls turn old at bars. Must be tiring. Twelve hours of your day spent walking the line between giving a guy just enough hope of a fuck that he'll tip, but beating him down when he goes over the edge.

"You got food?" I asked her, my stomach waking up to tell me that it had been empty since before Mexico.

She hands me a menu and I order the first item I see. "And double whiskey."

She puts in my order and gives me a once over. "You look like you've had a shitty day."

"I'm just here for this." I tell her, knocking back the whiskey from the glass that she hands me.

The girl tries not to show it, but a flash of 'asshole' passes over her face. That's bad for me. I don't want my drinks watered down. I reach into my pocket and hand her four times what the whiskey's worth. I give her the 'sorry' smile; "Yeah. Long day."

She takes the money, hands me another glass, and moves to the other end of the bar where a group of guys in their twenties take turns looking back and forth from her ass to Sports Center.

I see my burger and fries appear from a small window in the counter. The server sets it down in front of me. I don't catch what she said under her breath but I'm pretty sure it was "don't choke." For the first time in days I almost smile. Instead I stuff the food into my mouth like it's my last meal. Maybe, with what I've been thinking over the last few hours, it will be.

Then, in the mirror between the shelved bottles, I see the shape of someone coming to sit beside me. There's a lot of empty seats. I put down what's left of my burger and look at her. Say nothing.

She's blonde. Thin. Maybe twenty five. One look in her eyes and you know she's made some bad decisions in her young life. I guess she wants me to be the next one;

"Not interested."

She laughs and moves closer. I've never seen this girl in my life but I've met her a thousand times. They'd come from miles to hit the Ranger bars, especially when we got back from deployment. I don't know much about genes and DNA, but I think some people have 'fuck a killer' in theirs.

"I'm Cassie."

I go back to my food. She reaches out and traces her fingers over the ink on my knuckles, reading out the letters: "R. L. T. W. Is that gang ink?"

"You could say that."

She likes it. Her hand closes on top of mine. I'm trying to think of a polite way to tell her to get the fuck off of me when I hear a stranger's voice.

"Go suck a cock in the stalls, sweetie." The voice is as flat as Texas, and the girl doesn't fuck with it. She leaves, I stand, and look down at a familiar face. A *welcome* face.

"Sarah."

"Dom."

She hugs me. I know it's as unusual for her as it is for me, but it's not everyday that her brother dies.

She steps back. She wears black-rimmed glasses, but I see no tears behind them. She was Ethan's sister, but their relationship was about as strong as mine and the bartender's.

"I couldn't talk him out of it." I said. "Not this time."

She gestures for me to follow her to a booth. I do. She has that way about her. A leader. Sarah was a Rodeo champion at age thirteen and an FBI Agent a decade later. She knows how to lead a bull by the nose.

"Why not this time?" She asks me, knowing that it was me who'd kept Ethan tied to the earth long enough for him to meet Lucia.

"It was a woman."

"She left him?"

I didn't see the need for details. Not yet. I nodded.

She leaned back in the booth. Took a second to think that over. "I'll never understand you guys." She shakes her head. "You'll walk through bullets and IED's, but get your heart broken and you throw the towel in. I just don't understand it."

She has a point. I say nothing. The silence grows. It makes me itch. "How's Dallas?"

She makes a laughing sound, like she has no idea. "I just sleep there. But work? Work's… interesting."

"Anything you can talk about?"

She looks at my empty glass, "Maybe," and she signals to the server. I didn't need to ask her to know that it's going to be a long night.

CHAPTER 11

The bartender is avoiding me like I have Ebola, and so our booth table is slowly being covered with empties.

"Impressive." Sarah says, surveying the damage. Behind her glasses, her eyes are beginning to narrow from the booze, the slightest slur becomes present in her speech.

"I don't know where you put it." I tell her honestly. She can't be taller than 5'4".

"In my balls." She laughs, grabbing her crotch. "You fucking pussy."

And there it is. I laugh. It came and went faster than Christmas in Baghdad, but it was there.

Sarah looks at me with a triumphant look on her face. "Gotcha." She sits back. "I told myself I wouldn't ask you this until I'd gotten you to laugh."

There's no trace of humor in her voice now.

"You can talk to me, Sarah. You were his sister."

"Right." She reaches for her glass. Groans when she sees that it's empty. "So why didn't he come to me?"

It's a natural question with even

more natural reasons. Ethan grew up around cowboys and ranch hands before he became a Ranger and went to war. Do you think anyone ever taught him to talk? Do you suppose he was shown another way of dealing with grief except with fists and liquor? Ethan was a product of his upbringing - his time - and he was more likely to try talking to aliens about his problems than his younger sister, no matter how tough she was.

"Maybe that's the problem." I said to her after I'd spoken the rest.

"What do you mean?"

"He always felt that he was weak for suffering after war. Seeing you kicking ass, and getting by after your parents…"

"You think it made him feel like less of a man?"

I didn't say anything. I didn't need to.

"If he was here I'd punch him in the throat." She promised. "He could have at least had the balls to tell me he was going to do it."

"How did you find out?"

"Hospital. He called in before he did it." She gave a sad, sick little smile. "Apparently he was apologetic as hell about what they'd find. The mess, and… fuck it."

I kept my mouth shut. Sarah looked at

my hand, squeezing my glass.

"Ease up before you shatter that thing." And then she read the letters on my knuckles. "R. L. T. W."

"Rangers Lead The Way."

She looked up into my eyes. Hers were dark, and troubled. "Well, Dom, where are you going to lead me to tonight?"

CHAPTER 12

Her answer was a small motel a block down the street.

"I'll check in with you I tomorrow." I told her. "It's been good seeing you."

Sarah didn't seem to mind that she was going to bed alone. If anything, I felt like she was smug, and that I'd passed some kind of test.

"You can't drive home." She said, but there was nothing in the words that sounded like an offer to come inside.

"My place is a short walk from here." I lied. "I'm good."

We hugged and I walked away. I'd only taken a few steps before I heard the door to her room close. Grief makes people do stupid things, but I couldn't help shake the feeling that she'd been testing my character.

I looked into the bar parking lot and thought about driving. It would be a stupid idea at the best of times, but with my windows smashed in I was just asking for a cop to point a gun in my face before handing me a DUI.

My place was an hour's walk on the roads, but I wasn't a stranger to offroading it, and I've got a good sense of direction, even when I'm drunk. I started out on the hard packed dirt, a clear desert sky giving me all the illumination I needed.

I took the dip can from my jeans pocket and packed a thick lip. I wanted to sharpen up. I still had a lot to think about, and I was grateful that Sarah was in town. With her present to handle Ethan's affairs, I could concentrate on what was really important; finding and killing the people who had taken Lucia.

I ran through those plans for the first two miles as I marched across the desert. I was deep in thought, and if it wasn't for an unguarded flashlight I might have walked right on top of them.

I dropped to one knee, and controlled my breath. I knew I hadn't imagined seeing a stab of light cut out across the terrain, and after thirty seconds of waiting I saw it again. Judging the distance of light in darkness is never easy, but I estimated they were about the length of a football field away. Then, as my breathing and pulse quietened down, and I tuned into the night around me, I began to make out the faintest traces of voices.

All at once, I realized I was totally alert, and sober. I could smell opportunity here, and knew without doubt that whatever was out there in the night had been delivered to me for a reason. I wouldn't miss out on it, and I began to crouch and edge my way forward, careful to pick up and place my feet to avoid kicking rocks or dry vegetation. The light and voices were moving, but slowly, and heading north. That was about as much information as I needed to be certain that they were either mules, or more likely illegals who had just jumped the border a few miles to the south. Either way, I was eager to meet them.

Why? Because of my job as a border agent? Fuck no. Because Lucia had been taken by kidnappers, and if anyone knows the latest intelligence on that kind of criminal, it's the people running for their lives across the border.

Like a pit-viper I stalked my prey in the desert, creeping closer until they were within striking distance. From the voices I knew that there were at least three of them, and they all sounded scared. No voice of authority, which was good for me; the Coyote had probably already dumped them, and so I wouldn't have to kill him, and deal with a body.

The group had no idea that I was within ten yards of them. Their flashlight came on again, and I saw they were using it look at a shitty home drawn map. I waited until the light went out, and moved at once, striking while their eyes were still robbed of night vision.

Poor fuckers. Imagine it. You're already terrified, and then, from out of nowhere in the middle of a fucking desert you feel a 250-pound wrecking ball slam into your back. I used no words. I just threw myself into them, slamming bodies to the floor.

There was a lot of screaming. Then there was running. At the end of it, I had one of them pinned to the floor like some discovery channel shit. She was an adult women; I'd let the easiest target - the one kid in the group - go because there's nothing on earth that fights like a mother for her child. Instead, seeing that she was caught, she'd yelled at her kid to run and not look back. How fucking desperate were these people? Desperate enough to answer my questions, I hoped.

"Do you want to see your child again?" I asked in Spanish.

She did.

"I'll let you go." I promised. "I just want some answers. I'm going to get up now. If you move, I'll shoot you in your stomach and leave you to die here."

I moved. She didn't.

"Tell me everything you know about kidnappers in Juarez."

CHAPTER 13

It was a long night for me. Probably felt a lot longer for the illegal. I had to poke, and prod, but she sang, and I got my answers before letting her run terrified into the desert. Now I was sitting on the porch of my ranch, looking at a notebook in my lap. Everything she had told me, written down as soon as I'd come out of the desert with the dawn. There were routes, gangs, rumors, and whispers, but one name had my attention, and was circled in ink.

Lopez.

The name had come up again and again from my "informant." It had been said with the kind of fear I believe would be caused by a reputation for torture, like I'd seen inflicted on Lucia's body. So far as I could tell, Lopez was my man.

I lower the notepad, and think about going into the office to see what I can dig up on him there. The problem is, our job is more concerned with stopping people getting *in* than it is about looking out for the ones who get kidnapped and held across the border. That's the FBI's job.

I think about it for ten minutes before I call Sarah. I don't want her involved, but I decide to test the waters. The motel manager seems pissed that I interrupted him in the early hours to put the call through, but I don't have her cell, and I don't give much of a fuck about his jerking-off schedule.

"Hello?" She answers with the croak of the chronically hungover. "Oh, hey Dom. Jesus-fuck my head is killing me."

Now isn't the time to get her on my team. Sarah's always been a pro at whatever she does, and she's not about to put her career on the line without the biggest of reasons. I'm not sure yet how far I'm willing to bring her in, so I ask her to meet me that evening. When she asks what it's about, I tell her "Ethan's last wishes," but leave out the detail about how that included killing everybody who had harmed Lucia.

I hang up the phone and sit back in my chair. I'm beat up from emotions, a night in the desert, dehydration, and no sleep. I want to just close my eyes and sleep, but those Ranger School memories are there to poke me in my eyeballs; it's when you want sleep the most that you have to fight it. Your body is a weapon, and water and calories are its ammunition. I push myself up and out of the chair, and open the door into my kitchen.

It's then that I hear the *sicario*.

CHAPTER 14

The sound comes through the far wall; distinctive creaking of a footstep on the dry hardwood floor that needs oil. That's my bathroom, and some piece of shit is waiting in there so that he can put two rounds through my head before cutting me up in the tub. He knows who I am, how much I weigh, and is trying to save himself the job of dragging my ass in there from the kitchen, where he should have dropped me the second I opened the door. I draw my weapon; that bit of laziness is going to cost him his life.

I know what I *should* do here. I know what the play is - sit back. Call in the cavalry. Surround him. Take him alive.

The problem is, I've been itching to put holes in a motherfucker since Ethan first told me that Lucia'd been taken. I'm gonna gut-shot this piece of shit. I'll get answers, and my trigger squeeze too.

I've taken two steps towards the door when I hear the toilet flush. I stop in my tracks. No fucking way that a sicario just took a shit in my bathroom. And flushed! I hear the faucet run, and somebody washes their hands. I keep my weapon drawn, covering the door, and then it opens.

It's a kid.
It's Diego.

CHAPTER 15

That poor fucking kid. There he was, minding his business and taking a shit, and then he comes out of the bathroom to find me with God only knows what kind of look on my face, and a pistol pointing at his. Good thing he already went.

I lower the pistol instantly, but he's already starting to shake. I've seen grown ass men burst into tears or fill their pants when they come face to face with the business end of a gun. So I know I gotta reassure him, and quick. I cross the short distance to him, put my hands on his shoulders, and give him the most reassuring smile that I can.

"Hey, buddy!" I probably look like Shrek on molly, but I need to keep his mind so busy that it doesn't have a chance to process the thought that he was a split second away from getting wasted. "I'm so happy to see you! You want some breakfast? Come on, let's get some breakfast! Man, what a nice surprise!"

A hell of a fucking surprise.

I lead him toward the table and have him take a seat, then I'm over to the fridge like Martha fucking Stewart. "Milk, buddy? Eggs? I got pancake mix. Yo, what about pancakes, and eggs?"

I look at the young kid's face, and realize he's looking at me like I'm a crazy person. I drop the cookery act. Back to the Dom he knows. "Diego, why did you come here?" I ask him in Spanish, hoping that he's been spared the news, and this is a tragically timed 'fuck my parents, I'm running away' move.

He looks shaken. "I can't find my mom and dad. There's no one at home."

"Aren't you supposed to be with your Dad in Juarez?"

The kid shakes his head. "I was in El Paso with mama. She was talking with some people, and told me to wait where I was when she went with them."

I didn't need him to tell me that she didn't come back, but something he said stabbed at me; Lucia had been taken on this side of the border, not in Mexico. I didn't want to spook the kid, but he read the question on my mind anyhow.

"She looked scared."

I tried not to show any emotion, instead running over the math. This must have been days ago. "You didn't go straight to Ethan's?"

Diego nodded, almost guiltily. "I waited like she said, all day, but when it got dark I got scared. I tried to make my way to Ethan's, but then a cop on the road saw me walking and shouted at me. And I didn't want to get sent back to Mexico without my mom, so I ran."

I shook my head. Jesus. "How the heck did you find this place?"

"Dad brought me here to shoot." He said, and my heart pumped to hear him describe Ethan that way. I remembered those days as fondly as the kid, watching my brother teaching Diego with patience and pride. A ghost of a good memory pulled the corners of his mouth up into a smile. "I was on the road with the billboard for the sexy girls." He grinned coyly. "We always pass it on our way here, and I remembered the way from there. I'm not in trouble, am I?"

I crossed the kitchen to him and ruffled the kid's dark hair. "No buddy, you're not in trouble." I looked down at him, and my heart was torn between pity for him, and beating anger towards the people who had thrown this boy's life to the wolves. "You ready for some breakfast?" I asked him.

He did. But he also wanted something more.

"Uncle Dominic…" He asked me when his plate was clean. "Are my mom and dad okay?"

I know I have to tell him, but I don't know how, not yet. Instead I look for distraction. Anything.

"Did you bring any things with you? Clothes? Toys?" It's a stupid question, but maybe I can distract him by promising to take him to get some once the stores open.

"Only this." The kid says, getting to his feet so that he can pull something from his pocket. It's stuffed in tight, and he works to get it free with the same kind of effort King Arthur had to use for the sword in the stone.

"Got it." He says, handing it over to me.

I look down at what's in my hands. I've seen it before. You could say it was my last happy memory. I was drinking beers with my brother, watching Lucia and Diego painting a Sugarman mask for the Day of the Dead celebrations.

Diego sees the look in my eyes.

He smiles.

"It's for you."

CHAPTER 16

After eating everything in the fridge, I fall asleep on the sofa with Diego beside me. I'm not worried about unwanted visitors. I've thought it over. Aside from the usual Border Patrol danger, there's no reason to think that I'm in any more shit than usual. I could drop everything right here if I wanted to. Life could bump along like it always had. I'd need to figure out what to do with the kid, though. His dad's not an option, and I still haven't told him that the parents he loved are waiting for their patch of dirt.

Shit.

Diego's illegal so I don't need to worry about anybody missing him. He's good here for now. He is sleeping peacefully as I get up off the couch and go take a shower. I feel like shit but the presence of the kid has at least done something to persuade me that God hasn't abandoned me. He's given me some peace, and now I need to put my plan into action to see that others get theirs.

I find something in the freezer that the kid can eat for dinner, then do my best to gently wake him up. "I've gotta go out for a while."

He doesn't say anything but he doesn't look too stoked on the idea. At least not until I hand him the remote. "There's Netflix on there. Watch whatever you want."

His eyes go a little wide. "Anything?"

"Anything." If Piranha 3DD isn't in the recently viewed list when I get back, then I guess I don't know boys.

I head outside to my 'garage', which is just some tin roof on poles. The truck's space is empty, but my dirt bike is here. I kick up the stand and hit the long driveway out of my ranch.

I bought this place with a VA home loan and the money from my fourth deployment in 2009. Juarez was the most dangerous city in the world at the time, and a lot of people were bailing out, or at least not buying. This ranch belonged to an older guy who'd kicked ass in Korea, and he was worried that it would find its way to a straw buyer for the cartels, who were always looking for legitimately owned land for illegitimate purposes this side of the border. After we talked a bit about killing bad guys, he gave me this place for a steal. I wish the guy was around now. Wouldn't say no to a salty old vet like him watching my back.

I had had plans for the ranch. Family, first and foremost, but I fucked that one up before all of the others. When you don't like to think, being alone on a ranch isn't your friend. Thank God for the Border Patrol.

I turn out of my property and hit what isn't much more than a dirt road. I follow it almost all the way to the bar before I hit good asphalt, and with a lot of swearing and grunting, I get my bike loaded into the bed of my truck.

A couple of minutes later, I'm outside of Sarah's motel. She's waiting for me in the shade, a cigarette down to its last drag. "You look like you just shit an elephant." She tells me as she stubs it out on the wall.

"So what's this all about?"

I don't answer her. Not directly. "What would you have done for your brother?" I ask instead.

"If he'd have ever got over himself enough to ask me?" She grunts with a pained laugh, but then she sees something in my eyes, and holds my look. "Anything." She says, and I believe her.

"Let's take a drive."

CHAPTER 17

We don't talk as I drive. Sarah gets that this is no road trip, and that our destination is the place for answers. We get off the road and bounce across the country landscape, Sarah following me out into the shimmering heat and the stillness of the desert.

"This way." I tell her. "Almost there." I say, because the words are a distraction to myself. I don't want to remember the last time I was here.

She follows to my side. Out of the corner of my eye I see her face is neutral. No outward signs of the questions she must surely have building up inside her.

We finally come to the river. It breaks the silence of the desert, and I break my own.

"I found her here." I say, turning to face her. "The woman that your brother loved."

I see the corners of her eyes lift. The corners of her mouth fall.

She says nothing.

I tell her everything.

CHAPTER 18

I pull my truck to a stop outside of my house. For a moment I sit behind the wheel. Have I made the right decision?

I told Sarah I was going to tell her everything, and that was the truth, and a lie. I told her everything about how her brother had met and fallen in love with an illegal woman. I told her about how Lucia had taken his dark life and bathed it in light. I told her about how Lucia had been kidnapped, found dead, and that the final tragedy was too much for the man who had loved her more than life itself. I left out that she - *they* - had a son. And I left out that I planned on finding the people responsible, and killing them all.

"Why are you telling me this?" She asked, knowing that I wasn't doing it to help her fill out Ethan's obituary.

"I want the people responsible." I'd told her. "But you know how things work down here. She was here illegally, and he was a veteran with PTSD. I can't see them starting a task force over either of them, can you?"

She'd shaken her head. "So you're it?"

"I'm it. And I could really use your help."

And then I'd told her how. It wasn't her field, but Sarah would call in some favors and get me everything she could on the kidnap racket in El Paso and Juarez.

After all that, we'd stood in silence. I could tell there was a question she needed to ask. When she did, it wasn't the one I was expecting.

"Did Ethan come to you straight away?"

I hesitated. Thrown off. "No."

"Did he go to the police?"

Another pause. "No."

Then it was Sarah's turn to stall. "Do you think that…"

"He killed her himself, and this is a cover up?" I said it with more heat than I should have. Sarah didn't get defensive.

"War changes people. Could it have changed him?"

I shook my head. "Not like that." I wanted to tell her about Diego, and how he'd seen his mom leave with strangers, but the fewer people who knew about him for now, the better. I didn't want loose lips seeing him taken away and shipped back to his junkie dad.

Thinking of the boy, I left the truck running for the AC and walked onto the porch. "Diego!" I called out, and he came running to the door so quick that I expected to see a tail wagging.

"Uncle Dominic!"

"Hey kid." I said, a little taken aback at the enthusiasm. "Come with me. Let's go have some fun."

He smiled back at me, and in his eyes I saw the reflection of his mother's soul. The kid didn't know it, but I swore in that moment that tonight, people would bleed for her.

CHAPTER 19

When I was at war, the hours before a mission would be spent prepping gear, and doing rehearsals. Tonight, it was spent eating cheeseburgers and shooting zombies at an 'entertainment restaurant'. Diego was kicking my ass, but at least I was getting some trigger time.

"I suck at this." I told him. "You wanna try the basketball games?" Tall as I was, I'd gotten okay at hoops in the military thanks to killing hours on concrete around the world.

I spotted a net amongst the lights and led Diego to it, arriving at the exact same moment as what I guessed was a mom and her son. She was tall herself, north of 5'10", with an athletic physique. The kid was a bit older than Diego, and as blonde as her.

"I'm sorry," I said, feeling like we'd cut them off, "after you."

"Oh not at all." She smiled back, in an American accent I couldn't pin down. "There's two lanes. Why don't we let the kids go?"

She widened her eyes as she said it, as if to say "please God I need a break."

"Sure." I smiled. "Hey, Diego. Why don't you guys make friends?"

He beamed back at me, and he probably thought that life was rosy and that mom and dad would be joining us soon. How could that kid and this woman have any idea that I was just seeing this meeting as the perfect opportunity to help build an alibi? If something went wrong tonight and I got picked up by the law, a jury would have a hard time believing that Mr. Smiley at the restaurant had gone on to slit throats later that night.

"I'm Dom."

"Anna-Maria. This is Brad. My friends are on date night, so I guess they're trying to make him a brother or sister."

I hadn't met many blonde Anna-Maria's in my life, and she saw me raise my eyebrows, and laughed. "I take after my dad's side," she told me. "Big time. And my mom is Argentinian."

"I bet there's a story behind that." I said politely.

"Oh, you know, that old one about a naval ship coming into port and a sailor knocking up a local girl. The usual romantic tale."

This time my laugh was genuine.

"You were military yourself," she said, and it wasn't a question.

"Ranger. How'd you know?"

"You have that look."

"And what kind of look is that?"

"Like you used to be jacked, but not

enough to be a pro-athlete."

Fuck, she made me laugh again. "Damn. You nailed it."

She pretended to shoot for the hoop. "Don't give me too much credit. I grew up around it. Little Creek, Virginia."

"Your Dad was a SEAL?"

"He was, yeah." And something in her tone said that he was no longer walking the earth.

"Hey." She said quickly. "I've got to drop him off and get to a meeting, but…"

I saw where she was going, and spared her the embarrassment. "Here's my number," I said, handing her one of my Border Patrol cards. "Meetings at this time, huh? Savage."

She shrugged. "I'll tell you about it sometime, Agent Dominic De Leon." She said, reading my card. "Border Patrol, huh?"

I felt there was an edge to her words, but in a split second her smile was back. "I better get going. Nice to me meet you, Agent De Leon."

She took the kid's hand and walked away. I felt Diego's eyes on me. "Can we shoot more zombies?"

I looked at my watch, and shook my head. The time for games was over. Outside, darkness was falling.

And I was coming with it.

CHAPTER 20

Night has come, and it's time for me to go. I was worried about getting Diego to sleep, but the kid was out of it as soon as we got back to the house. I told him that I've got to work tonight. That's true enough, in a sense.

I collect the few tools that I need and place them in a ruck. I pull it onto my shoulders, the weight giving me comfort, but I'm stopped on my way to the door by something on the kitchen table; Diego's Sugarman mask.

"Fuck it." I pick it up, and put it into my jacket pocket.

I take the dirt bike, hitting the roads first before I break track and kill the lights. I pull a helmet with mounted night vision from my ruck, and cover the next couple of miles cross country, my eyesight back to the familiar green shades of my wartime service. I know this territory well, and I hide the bike under thick brush - I'll be covering the last two miles on foot.

I use a weak red light to check my position on my GPS as I head south, closer to the border. Google Earth has given me the top down look I need, and now it's seared into my mind as I check off landmarks. It's not long before I see what I came for; a low black shape peeking up on the dark horizon. It doesn't look much like it did when I was handed a photo in the briefing room, but this is my target; the cartel tunnel.

CHAPTER 21

The building that housed the suspected tunnel was an agricultural outbuilding that had seen better days. Likely it had fallen into disuse because it was so close to the border, not three hundred yards away. A rancher would be too worried about leaving equipment in there with how things were these days, and maybe the cartel had spotted an empty building and moved in. More likely they'd sent in somebody half-respectable looking to buy it, and the rancher was either blinded by ignorance, or by dollars.

I couldn't see any lights as I watched the building from a slight rise a hundred yards away, but I didn't expect to either. They'd have covered the windows on the inside, because the night was when they did a lot of their work. Sure, the Border Patrol had thermal cameras, but you need eyes to watch a screen, and we just didn't have enough. Usually I cussed about that kind of thing, but tonight it was in my favor. The only eyeballs I wanted on what I was about to do were in skulls south of the border.

I crawled a few yards backward, then to my right, and into a depression in the ground I made a final check on the tools that I had in my ruck; I'd chambered a round in the pistol when I was out of the range of sound for the building, so I simply pushed my palm against the slide to check that the hollow-point round inside was sitting snug. I slid it into the holster on my hip. Next I lifted a Mossberg 500, and put the sling over my head and shoulder. I'd removed the stock, and she lay comfortably along my side. Finally, I reached down and picked out what I'd seen lying on my kitchen table; Diego's Sugarman mask. I pulled it over my head, whispered a prayer to my brother Ethan, and stepped out toward the building.

CHAPTER 22

I crossed the open ground quickly, an AR-15 up to my shoulder. If I got into the shit before I entered the building, this is what I'd use to get out of it, but everything was quiet as I slipped toward the one story structure. There was a truck outside, but no signs of life, and I thought that maybe I could make a silent entry before I heard the fucking dog begin to bark.

Forget your ten thousand dollar intruder alarms. A dog is the best system on the planet, and this one was trying to fuck up my evening. With all hopes of stealth now out the window, I pushed the AR on its sling around my back, and lifted the Mossberg.

I was about to blast off the hinges and kick through the door when something stopped me. By starlight, through a missing sliver of wood, I'd caught the slightest of shines of light reflecting off metal; they'd reinforced the door, and the dog was still fucking barking. *Fuck*.

Nothing to do but to improvise, adapt, and overcome. I looked around me, and saw something that would work.

I ran to the truck just as I heard

the first sounds of voices inside. They didn't sound happy. For a split second I considered sitting back and hoping I could pick them off as they came out to investigate, but I needed answers more than I needed bodies. No. I needed to get into that building, and I needed to do it now.

I tried the truck door and it came open. Struggling with my size and the kit that I had on, I pushed myself inside, and tried the obvious places for keys. No luck, but I grew up poor, angry, and lost, and the truck was old. No sweat.

I hot-wired it, then put it into reverse, lurching back forty yards from the building. Far enough. I took one more look over the dash to check my aim, then laid down across the seats as I mashed the accelerator.

CHAPTER 23

The door was reinforced but the walls weren't, and the truck hit them like JJ Watt, showering down timber and plaster as it plowed half-way through the wall before getting caught up on debris. My eyes were assaulted for a second by light, the inside of the building lit up electrically. I didn't want to give my hosts a second to recover, and so I lifted up the Mossberg and blasted out the windshield with the breaching rounds I'd had chambered, and then I put a few rounds of buckshot into the room to keep heads down as I opened the passenger door, and pulled myself out of it onto my front.

I didn't get shots back, only shouts, and I heard groans. Looking down beside me I saw the reason behind those; I'd parked the truck on top of a bad guy.

He had no weapons in his hands, and he wasn't going anywhere, so I left him to concentrate on his friends. I stood up in time to see a wide-eyed guy coming at me with a machete. I hit him with the Mossberg from two yards away and his chest disappeared. Speed, surprise, and violence of action where my allies in this fight and so I moved as quickly as I could from the truck, past the threadbare sofas and stacked pallets which I guessed held their product. A couple of rounds snapped at me from a doorway up ahead and I dropped the Mossberg and pulled my AR into my shoulder. The guy had thought he was behind cover, but a plaster partition wall is no match even for 5.56, and I drilled several double taps through it before moving forward. That was three bad guys accounted for, and I had no idea how many could be in here; I needed at least one alive, and I couldn't count on my buddy the valet to hang on long enough to give me answers.

It was thinking about that, and not my room clearance, that gave the big guy behind a pallet the split second he needed to grab the end of my AR. He was a strong mother fucker and pulled the barrel down toward the floor, where his leverage would be at its strongest, and mine was at its weakest. He knew it, and the big fuckers eyes were wild with 'fuck you' excitement as he kept his weight on the weapon, and tried to bite my face.

I knew that thanks to physics, he had all the advantage in our wrestling match, and so I threw in the towel, and surrendered the weapon. His hands were on the barrel, not the trigger, and by the time he'd realized I'd let go, I'd drawn my pistol, placed it to the side of his head, and blown his brains all over what he was supposed to be protecting.

The big fuck didn't die in vain though. He'd bought his buddies time to rally, but from the sounds of the panic, they'd decided to retreat instead. Fuck that. I followed the two of them through the partition and saw them hurriedly pulling back the metal sheeting that covered their tunnel entrance. In desperation to save their lives they'd dropped their weapons to use both hands; I had my prisoners.

"Put your hands up!" I ordered in Spanish. "Stop moving! Hands up! Now!"

One of them, an older guy with a leather face, did as I said immediately. The other was so panicked that he didn't know which way to look, but when I saw his eyes go to an AK a couple of yards away. I didn't waste any more time, and put a double-tap into his chest. The blood hit Leather Face, but he kept his hands up; a good sign.

"Want to live?"

"Si senor."

"On your knees. Hands on the back of your head." He complied. "How many of you here?"

"Six, senor."

I'd accounted for that many. Now that the ringing of my last shots had left the room, the only thing I could hear were the groans coming from my parking space. I had a choice; sweep the building inch by inch, and risk the cavalry - or worse, law enforcement - arriving, or take my chances that there could be someone hiding, and keep speed on my side.

I choose speed.

"Tell me everything you know about Lopez, the kidnapper."

"I don't know anything about --"

I cut him off by putting a round into his friend's head. The guy was already dead, but there's something about seeing a skull crack open that loosens lips.

He talked. I listened.

"Is there money here?" I asked him. He nodded and gestured to a crate on the far side of the room.

I walked to the front of the man, and looked into his face. I saw terror, but did I have sympathy for that? He had chosen a life where terror and pain were the currency. I almost wanted to ask him why. Why this? Why the cartel? I couldn't shake the feeling - the voice - telling me that this guy hadn't grown up wanting to be a mule for a drug gang. That he had wanted more from life.

Fuck it.

"What did you want to be when you were a kid?" The killer in the Sugarman mask asked him, pointing a gun at his face. "When you grew up. What did you want to be?"

He stammered an answer. This question seemed to spook him more than any other. Maybe he'd realized that my questions were over, and with them, the need to have him alive.

"I wanted to be a race car driver." The guy stuttered.

I almost laughed. Not at him, but just at…

Everything. Neither of us had grown up wanting to be in a room that now stank of blood and death.

"I wanted to be wrestler." I told him honestly. "You remember Hulkamania?"

"Please don't kill me…"

"Lie on your front. Keep your hands behind your head."

"Please, sir, please don't kill me." He begged, but he did as I told him, and then I pressed my knee into his back.

"I need you to take a message back to Mexico." I said, and I felt his relief shake through his body.

Then I felt his agony, as I cut off his fingers and thumbs.

CHAPTER 24

There was something about Leather Face that had made me not want to kill him, but I had probably killed his dream of being a race car driver by cutting off his trigger fingers and thumbs; I'd heard the French used to do it to captured archers back in the day, and it made a lot of sense. Why let someone with a grudge against you hold a weapon?

I'd sent Leather Face into the tunnel, and then I'd helped myself to a duffel bag of cash. By the time that I'd gotten back to the truck my valet was dead, and I didn't have to hear him scream as I backed out through the wall. I did go back to him though. Trying not to look too much at the wheel rut I'd left across his torso, I placed a roll of money in his hand. I didn't do it for my amusement, but because I wanted people to talk. I wanted Lopez to know that there was a psycho in a Sugarman mask out there who drove trucks over people and then tipped them like the world's best valet. I wouldn't want that guy coming after me, and with a guy who's into his sick fucking torture like Lopez evidently was, then you've gotta get inventive to get his attention.

I loaded the truck up with what I needed, and took a short drive. I went back and forth for the next twenty minutes, and by the time that I did it I was soaked with sweat, but I knew my message was sent.

It was time to get the fuck out.

CHAPTER 25

Tracking back to my ranch I throw in misdirections and stops to make sure I'm not being followed before placing my weapons into heavy duty trash bags and burying them in a cache in the desert. I've used them all, so they all have to go, at least for now.

When I get home I strip and put my clothes in a barrel, soak them with gas, and light it up. I look at the Sugarman mask in my hands, know that I should burn it, but I can't bring myself to throw it into the flames. I just can't. I don't know why. I've never been much of a sentimental type. Maybe that's the point.

Instead I put it into my fresh pants and check in on Diego. Kid's flat out on the couch, but Netflix is still on the TV. I don't see Piranha 3DD in the recently viewed. Instead it's superhero after superhero. Maybe I should buy him some comics?

I shake my head. I'm playing happy lives with the kid, but the truth is that his is fucked. I don't even know if I'm going to make it out alive in keeping my promise to Ethan. Shit, do I even want to? Right now I've got a mission. I've got a cause. I've got purpose. What happens when that goes away and it's just me, myself, and my thoughts. Maybe Ethan knew what he was doing.

Snap out of it.

I sit back into an arm-chair. I make sure my phone is on loud, and sitting on my chest. I close my eyes, and try to sleep before the coming shit storm breaks.

CHAPTER 26

I haven't been out for more than forty minutes before my phone begins to bark at me. My eyes feel like they've been glued together. I open them with the back of my hand, and look at the screen; the office.

"Yo?"

"Hey, Dom." I recognize the voice of Ortega. "Sorry, were you asleep?"

"No, no, just dozing. What's up?"

"I know you're not in until tonight, but…" *but I know you that don't have a life, and you live for this shit,* "remember that tunnel house we thought we might have?"

Yes, Ortega, you could say I remember it. "Yeah. What about it?"

"It got hit last night."

"Hit?"

"*Hit.*"

I do my best to sound confused. "What, like, by our guys?"

I can almost hear the sound of awe down the phone. If there's one thing Agent Ortega likes, it's dead cartel. "Why don't you come out take a look?"

"Okay. Sure."

"Great. I'll text you the location. And bring me a coffee, would you?"

"Sure, popcorn too?"

Ortega laughs. "You're not gonna have much of a stomach when you see this mess."

He hangs up, and I get to my feet. Time to go look at my handy work.

CHAPTER 27

The scene of the crime is crawling with law enforcement, most of them with hard-ons. Some are working what's now a murder case, but a lot have just come down here to see dead bad guys. In many ways the cartel are an invisible enemy like the ones I fought overseas, and so it gives people a nice fuzzy feeling to see one with their skull split open.

"What the fuck happened to your truck?" Ortega asks me as I arrive.

"Mexico."

He doesn't say anything in reply. Just gives me a little smile, figuring there's only one reason for a single guy to be crossing south.

"Take a look at this." He gestures to me, and I walk with him to the body of the guy I'd crushed with the truck.

Ortega shook his head. "That's gotta be a thousand dollars in his hand."

I shrug. "How many of them?"

He gives me a guided tour of the place, all of the bodies where I left them. "Find any cameras?" I ask, knowing the cartels sometimes film their own men to keep them honest.

"None that we've found."

We walk to the body of the big guy that had grabbed my AR. He doesn't look any better dead than he did alive.

Ortega turns to me. "I don't know of anyone in El Paso who's kicked in more doors than you, Dom. What do you make of this? How many guys to pull it off? They must have come in with the truck, right?"

"Seems that way." I shrug. "I don't know, Orty. I've kicked in doors, sure, but I was a grunt. I wasn't ever in on the planning, and things."

"But to kill five guys and not lose anyone?" He presses me.

"How'd you know they didn't lose anyone?"

"Blood." He said as if it's obvious, but I shake my head.

"I've seen bodies that didn't leak more than a few drops. I wouldn't rule out that they took their dead away."

Ortega runs a hand over his chin, then nods. "We'll get blood samples anyway. See how many we can identify through that."

He doesn't get a chance to reply before Martin puts his head in through the door, looking like an excited puppy. "You gotta come see what we found in the river!"

CHAPTER 28

Martin leads Ortega, myself, and a half dozen others the short distance to the river. As we walk, the group tosses theories back and forth about who was responsible for the hit, and why.

"It's an inside job." Martin says with assumed authority. "They brought in outside help."

But when we get to the river, Ortega shakes his head. "If it's an inside job, then why'd he dump the coke in the river?"

The banks are littered with dead fish.

Martin's smile drops.

I've seen enough.

"You're out?" Ortega asks me as he sees me walk away.

"Got a date."

He slams his fist into his palm. "I fucking knew it!" He grins. "Where's she at?"

I smile back.

"Mexico."

CHAPTER 29

I'd been south of the border for three hours in a rented Camry. I'd picked the shittiest thing they had on the lot to try and avoid attention, and so far it was working. The AC was about as efficient as me flapping a hand in front of my face, but I wasn't complaining. Perspective is a powerful thing, and I knew that I could be a lot worse off.

The proof of that was down the street a hundred yards away. It was a safe house that Leather Face had told me about before I took his trigger fingers and thumbs. A place where Lopez's gang held their victims until ransoms were paid.

This area was not like the slum barrio that was home to Diego's junkie dad. This was middle class Juarez, with no one working corners, and regular police patrols. The residents pay for their protection, and I guess that includes Lopez. Without doubt he has a cartel umbrella, and that probably comes with police and politicians too. The all-inclusive scum bag package.

Just the thought of Lucia's kidnappers begins to bring a red mist over my eyes, and I think about pushing my thumbs into Lopez's eyes until I feel them burst. I've never wanted to kill anyone more in my life, or more slowly, but I do what I can to force the feelings away. Not because they make me uncomfortable, but because I want those dreams to become a reality, and the best way to make that happen is to keep cool, and stay vigilant.

I catch sight of movement in my rearview and see a police car slowly crest the hill that leads to the top of the street. I see two bored faces, just cruising, and they pull to a stop about fifty yards ahead of me as I do my best to sink my big frame back into the Camry.

The cops get out of their car and take a seat outside of the restaurant. They're totally nonchalant, one even with his back to the road. Either they're idiots, or this is a no-go zone. A spot that rival cartels have agreed to leave out of their turf wars so that their kids have a safe place to go to school, and their wives can get their nails done. There's no such thing as a war without rules, no matter what people tell you, and even the biggest *jefe* believes in happy wife, happy life.

The cops are sipping beers by the time the next vehicle of interest rolls down the street. Sometimes you just get a sense for things, and this one put my back up. Maybe it was the tint on the glass. Maybe it was the way it cut off a signaling car. It was a minivan driven with attitude, and when it passed by the cops, I saw the cops look at each other and say something. They knew, and they didn't want to know, and they stood up and took their beers inside.

It was no surprise to me then when the gates opened and the minivan pulled into the house that I had been told belonged to Lopez. On instinct I turned on the engine and pulled into the road, slowly cruising, not wanting to spook. The gates were almost closed by the time that I rolled by, but looking through them I saw enough; a gagged woman was being dragged out of the mini-van by her hair, and led inside.

I had my next target.

CHAPTER 30

Some things that you see in life burn into your retinas, and as I drove back to El Paso for my shift at the agency, the kidnap victim being dragged by her hair was like a watermark across my vision. I tried to shake it. She wasn't my problem. But I couldn't help but think of what would happen to her. How she'd end up like Lucia. Maybe worse.

There's always worse.

I joined Border Patrol because I had too much time to think, and it saved me again this day. The tunnel takedown was still the hot shit on everyone's lips, but the daily grind hadn't stopped because of it. There were still illegals to round up. Mules to stop. Patrols to carry out. Paperwork to fill in. I wasn't the kind of guy who asked for days off, and I didn't want to break patterns, so I clocked in and out like it was any other day, and I didn't have blood on my hands, and plans for more to come.

My last job of the day was to process a couple of illegals who'd been picked up in town. They were young guys, their chins on their chest now that they knew they were going home.

"Please don't send us back, sir." One of them said to me in English. "It's a war."

I shook my head, and answered in Spanish. "Your home is your home."

He almost looked pissed. Again he spoke in English. Someone in your family wasn't born here. What about their home?"

I'd heard it before, and didn't reply. It's not like I didn't believe the kid had a point. As far as I knew from my dad, my grandpa had come to the States from Mexico during World War 2, when they needed immigrants to backfill the jobs left by men going off to fight. I didn't have answers for this kid. Instead I told him "Good luck," and left the building.

How could I have known I walking into an ambush?

CHAPTER 31

She was waiting for me right outside the door, a cigarette in her hand and a tired smile on her face.

"Anna-Maria." She looked like she'd clocked some miles since I saw her full of jokes at the kid's restaurant. "Hey."

"Hey." She dropped her cigarette and ground it out beneath a hiking boot. "Can I buy you dinner?"

I didn't know what to say to that. I had plans, and they involved looking into how best to kill people. My stomach had its own ideas though, and opened my mouth for me. "Sure, I'd love to."

We chatted small talk and bullshit as we walked to a bar a little down the street. "Have you eaten here before?" She asked me.

"All the time. Pulled pork burger's really good."

She pulled a face. "I'm Vegan."

"In Texas?"

"Yeah. Don't turn me in."

"We'll find you a pickle or something." I joked, regretting it instantly as I realized the innuendo.

"Don't threaten me with a good time." She laughed, and for a second she looked more like the woman I'd met the first time.

"Long day, huh?"

She took a seat at a table, and sighed. "Long fucking day. But then, they usually are."

I didn't say anything. I sensed this needed to be a one way conversation.

"I have a charity. I run a charity."

I let my silence ask her more.

"We help illegals." She paused here, waiting to see my reaction. There was none. "We give them water, food, all that kind of thing, and then we try and provide them with legal counsel. I say *try*, because, well, you know…"

Because the border's fucking overwhelmed, I thought, but instead I just nodded and said, "I know."

"There are good people in law enforcement." Anna-Maria said in a way that implied there were plenty of bad ones too. "I feel like we need to be pulling together more than we are. Everything feels so hostile, Dom." She said, looking more tired with every word. "When did we become these tribes and stop being *people*?"

I had no answer for her, and I was glad when the server came over to take our orders. I wasn't surprised that Anna-Maria went for a beer along with her vegetarian sides. I ordered my usual. I was here for fuel, nothing more.

I kept quiet after that, and after a moment, Anna-Maria filled the space. "It just feels like it's all point scoring, you know? Agencies feel like if they help us, they're losing in some game, and… and honestly, I know the feeling, because I've had it myself. We haven't bent on what we wanted sometimes, and I gotta ask myself, is it just because of pride? What are we doing here, Dom? *These are people.*"

She said my name, but I could tell the words were for her.

She needed to have this conversation out loud with herself, and I decided it was time to tell her as much.

"You're right." She said. "Fuck it, Dom, it's such a mess."

I expected she wanted more than my ear. "How do you think I can help?"

Our beers arrived. "Cheers." The glass bottles clinked, and she took half of hers down in the first pull. "You give a fuck, Dom. I can just tell. I don't know how we can help each other yet, but would you be open to me bringing things to you? Maybe we could work on packaging ideas together in a way that would get the agencies and law enforcement more likely to want to work together with us. I'm not stupid, and I know that the barriers are going to be up when it's coming from a vegan who's never worn a uniform in her life."

She smiled at that dig at herself. I took another sip of my beer. "I'll do what I can." And I didn't know if I was saying it because I wanted to end the conversation, because I did care, or because there was something in her blue eyes that was dangerous and magnetic. I couldn't put my finger on what it was. She seemed so caring, and gentle, but I've been around enough sharks to recognize the look, and she had it. Fuck. Even with the shit storm raging, I wanted to know more about this woman.

"So what are you doing tonight?" She asked me.

CHAPTER 32

Anna-Maria's eyes are promising me a lot. A lot of things that I want, but there's something I want more.

"I gotta go."

I see more surprise on her face than disappointment. She's beautiful, and by the looks of it, driven. This isn't the kind of thing that happens to her. "But I'll call you."

She shakes her head. "I'll call you."

That's probably the end of that, then. She's taken back control.

I pull some money from my wallet, but she holds up her hand; "I asked you out, remember?"

I don't push it. Just thank her, and leave. I've never been the kind of guy that women fall over themselves to get, but there's a certain kind of girl that I swear can smell damage, and it pulls them in. Some come to pick your bones clean, others to try and put you back together. Considering what she does with her life, I figure Anna-Maria's the second kind, but like all of us she's got an ego, and I probably just bruised hers. I doubt I'll hear from her again. Maybe just to tell me that I missed out.

I have twenty minutes to think about that as I drive across town to Sarah's motel, and knock on the door. She opens it in her workout gear, her arms and shoulders jacked. Exercise is medicine, and she's been drinking hers by the bottle.

We hug, and say hello. I figure I'm going to have to push her into what she's about to do, but I needn't have worried. She walks over to the bed, and picks up a file of papers. "This is everything I could get." She tells me. "Read it and burn it."

I take it with a nod. "I can do it here?" I tell her, knowing that this kind of thing ends careers, but she shakes her head.

"You were Ethan's brother."

I hold her look, then turn for the door. My hand's on the doorknob when she speaks to my back. "I heard about the tunnel house."

I say nothing. Don't move.

She continues. Her voice is calm, like she's talking about the weather. "No one knows who did it…"

I turn and face her. Hold out the files. "You don't need to give me these." I tell her. She knows, and she deserves a chance to bail.

She doesn't take it. "I know. She says. "Just be careful, Dom. Be really careful."

I turn back for the door, and step out into the sunlight. I'd walked into that room to an FBI Agent, and left her as an accomplice to murder. It wasn't just my ass on the line, now.

I stop at the door to my truck, and look at what's in my hands. It looks like a pile of papers, but to me, I'm seeing a rope to put around Lopez's neck.

Time to get to work.

CHAPTER 33

When I get home Diego is watching superhero movies. I ask him if he has everything he needs.

He doesn't.

"Where are my mom and dad, Uncle Dominic? Are they coming back soon?"

I scramble, and make up some bullshit about them having to visit a family member. "But you and me can have fun here, right?"

"Sure." And he smiles, but there's a look in his eyes of a kid that misses his mom. Those guys were joined at the hip, and he's hurting. How's he going to handle that the rest of his life? There's only so many superhero movies.

"Are you okay in here while I do some work in the kitchen?" I leave him under the supervision of the TV screen and place the folder Sarah had given me on the kitchen table. It was thin, but I wasn't looking for War and Peace, and I'd been specific in what I'd asked her to try and dig up; information on kidnap victims who had ties to family or loved ones in America. As a Ranger, we carried out relatively similar missions again and again with the same operating procedures, and I didn't think that the kidnappers would be any different. They'd find a formula that worked, and stick to it. I told myself that I'd read through the case notes once, and then come back through and write down any commonalities, but I was only five victims in when something jumped out at me; the next of kin of three of the first five victims were active military or veterans. I made a note of that, then continued to work through. The victims were almost all women, and like Lucia, they had been killed even after ransoms had been paid. Some were missing presumed dead because the ransom calls had stopped. Others had been found on both sides of the border, horrifically mutilated. It was hard for me to keep a check on my anger and stay focussed, but by the end of my second read of the pile I looked at my notes, and saw that that twenty-two of the forty-eight victims had next of kin that had served, or were serving, with the US Military.

    I thought about that for a second. Nearly half of the kidnapped and murdered women found in and around El Paso over the last year had either fathers, husbands, or brothers who had fought for Uncle Sam.

    I sat back in my chair. Folded my arms. Closed my eyes. It didn't take me long to come up with the answer; Texas was a military state. Over 10% of Uncle Sam's children came from here, and a lot of those are from closer to the border where it's harder to get low paying jobs that get taken up by migrant workers. As a kidnapper, you don't want the people you ransom to talk, and it stood to reason that veterans would be able to handle the pressure better than most, and come up with the money.

I closed the file and got to my feet, carrying it out to the empty burn barrel, the ashes long since scattered by me in the desert on my way out to the crime scene that morning. Now it was the turn of Sarah's guilt to burn, but as I added each page to the flame, I couldn't help but linger a look over the photo of each victim. I've seen a lot of death, and to some degree I think I've built my callouses, but the sight of a woman tortured turned my stomach. With each photo I saw, the memory of the victim I had seen getting dragged inside by her hair grew stronger. By the time that the last page was ash, my mind was made up.

I wouldn't let her die like the others.

CHAPTER 34

I had planned to wait. To plot. To plan. I wanted Lopez's head, but I knew I couldn't take him down in his place as easily as I had done with the tunnel house. It was in another fucking country, for one thing, but as much as I knew it was a bad idea, I knew that the thought of abandoning that girl to the same fate as Lucia was one that I couldn't stomach.

A loud voice in my head kept telling me I was booking myself a one way ticket to the dirt, and I couldn't disagree. I left Diego in the truck as I went to Sarah's motel for a second time that day, and told her about the boy who would one day have become her nephew.

"He needs a place to stay."

She didn't ask me where I was going. My eyes told her. I was never the life of a party, but before a mission there was a dark edge to my movement and tone. Emotion was stowed. My speech was clipped. There was an economy in my movement. It was like my body and mind were trying to save every last bit of energy in my cells for when I really needed it.

Sarah came over to the truck with me and introduced herself to Diego. He lit up when he found out who she was. I'd never seen Sarah cry, but in that moment I thought that I was about to.

"I'll take him inside. See you tomorrow." She didn't wait or look for a reply. She was gone, and I needed to be, too.

I drove my truck to where I'd left the Camry in town and switched cars. I hit the border as the sun was going down, splashes of violent red scattered across the horizon. For once I was glad of the unmoving traffic, and I drank in every second of the sunset.

I didn't expect that I'd ever see another.

CHAPTER 35

Midnight. Mexico. I'm back on Lopez's street. Parked, the opposite end in. No sight of cops drinking at the restaurant. There's a couple of guys stood outside there, smoking, but they look more like architects than bangers. The police patrolled this area in the day, so I know they'll be back in the dark, and I wait for them before I make my move. No bag of tools tonight. No night vision devices. I've bought a machete and a six inch kitchen knife from a hardware store. I could have run the risk of crossing the border with heat, but if I got pulled up then it's all over. Lopez lives, and *I* can't live with that. I'd rather risk my skin than the mission.

I lift the machete from down by my side and hold it low across my lap. I've used one to clear bush in the jungle, but never a guy's head. First time for everything, right? I used to have a squad leader who'd played Division One Football and he told me he used to visualize every play before every game. I'd picked up the habit in Iraq, but tonight the only thing I could visualize was that blade plowing down between Lopez's eyes.

I was too angry for this mission. Too involved. Too distracted. I didn't know who I was going up against. I didn't even know who I was trying to rescue, but that didn't matter. It never had. I sure as fuck hadn't been put on the planet to have a good time, so this must be it.

I see lights coming. Sink back into my seat. A cop car rolls by. I smell weed, and then they're gone.

I take one last look at my machete, and then I pull the Sugarman mask over my head.

CHAPTER 36

The six foot wall is topped with broken glass set into the structure, but nothing more, and it's easily taken out quietly by laying a thick pile of sacking across it. I still feel the glass pushing at me as I haul myself over, but nothing cuts.

I expect dogs on the other side, and I don't have a string of sausages in my pocket like the movies. If they come at me, I'll have to deal with them with a blade, and I'm not happy about that - either for me, or the dog - but I have no other choice; Cesar Millan couldn't make it along for this mission.

I see no cameras, but that means nothing. My best warning of my ambush will be my ears, because bad guys tend to get shouty when they're spooked; especially ones with a readily available supply of party drugs.

I cross the yard quickly and find some shadow against a wall. Stop and listen. So far no atmospherics in the neighborhood have changed. My breathing's a little more heavy from the wall, and in the distance I hear a gunshot, but that's Juarez as usual in a city that averages four murders a day - I could almost smile at that. No matter what happens in the next five minutes, no matter who dies, it's just going to be another stat in a war without end.

Satisfied that I haven't been seen - or that I'm about to walk into an ambush, and get a quick death at least - I move up to the nearest window. There are no bars on the outside, and I don't expect to see any on the inside, either; this is a nice neighborhood, protected by cartel and police, and the rich don't need to worry about ugly things on the windows when they have guys with guns in their employment.

I try the window, but it's locked from the inside. So are the next two that I try, and the others all have faint light behind the curtains. I move back to the first, furthest from them, and take a roll of tape from my jacket pocket, quickly applying it from side to side on the glass. Then I take out a spark plug, and as quietly as I can, I go to work on the corners of the pane using its hard ceramic end. The glass breaks, and held together with the tape, comes out in my hands. I place it down on the floor, and without giving myself a second chance to think about it, I enter the house with the machete in my hand.

CHAPTER 37

There doesn't seem to be any sounds of panic as I move inside of the house. I've come into a utility room, but none of the machines are running. I can hear a couple of voices, maybe a TV, but no sounds of tears or torture. From the work that I saw on Lucia's body, I figure that there must be a basement.

I'm split in my decision. I want to get to the kidnapped girl, but the rescue could be short lived if I don't deal with the people who took her. Bad guys sleep too, and it's late, so some of them will be in their beds.

I like killing bad guys in their beds.

I ghost out into the hallway. Everything about this home says upper middle class family. I wonder if they're in on it, or did they fall foul of the cartel, and the smiling people I see in the photos are out in the desert right now, but their mortgage keeps getting paid so the house can be used by Lopez and his gang…

I'm certain now that I can hear a TV, probably for the guys 'on watch', but I don't want to start a fight with them that will go noisy, and alert the people upstairs. Sleeping beauties first.

I creep up the stairs, careful to put my feet on either side of the boards where they're strongest, and less likely to make noise. For a split second an image flashes into my mind of the one time I'd tried to play Santa, but this is no time for memories, and I shake it out of my head.

Finding the first of the enemy isn't hard. The snoring sounds like someone's sawing logs. I quietly push open the door an inch, and see an overweight guy asleep in his boxers. He doesn't realize it, but his snoring has bought him an extra two minutes of life. I look into the next room, and see a younger guy tucked into the sheets, cartel ink on his arms and neck. There's a pistol by the bedside - a gift to me - and that's all the proof I need to convict him. I take a screwdriver from my pocket, and drive it into the base of his skull.

Next bedroom. This one's a woman. More ink. She looks like a tough bitch. She's asleep on her back. I have to think about the best way to take her out, standing over her like some kind of fucking demon. I pick up a piece of clothing and clap it over her mouth. Her eyes open wide and she tries to bite me, but the cloth stops her, and then I'm opening her neck with the knife. It's louder than I want to be, but

I have one pistol already, and once she's drained out into the mattress, I look for hers, and find a second semi-auto and a spare mag. I quietly chamber a round and then go back for the guy sawing --

Fuck. *The snoring's stopped.*

CHAPTER 38

Bits of plaster spray over me as a shotgun shell explodes through the wall. I dive across the bed just in time to miss the second blast, and before the third can come in I reach up for the dead woman, and pull her down on top of me. Hot blood runs onto my face and I feel the body jerk as round four, five, and six turn the bedroom into a hell of shrapnel.

Through the ringing in my ears I hear the frantic signs of reloading. I push the corpse off of me and get up to one knee, dumping a mag from left to right across the wall. I hear a grunt of pain, and I take that as my chance to move.

Fuck coming out through the door way. The shotgun has torn apart the wall and so I just put my shoulder to it as I run and crash through. The snorer is trying to get to his knees, clutching at his stomach, but I bring the machete down into his skull before he can reach back for the shotgun. I want that weapon but I don't see any more shells close at hand, and this isn't the time to look; shouts are coming from downstairs.

I change magazines and rack the slide. I turn to look down the staircase and punch the pistol out to scan for bad guys. As I expected there's the TV watching bad guy waiting, but his aim is loose and wild, and mine is tight. He goes down with two in the chest. My third shot missed his head, but my machete takes care of that as I pass him and move down into the basement.

Two seconds later, and I wished that I hadn't.

CHAPTER 39

At first I thought what I was seeing hanging from the basement ceiling was a pig's carcass, but then I saw the long hair, and realized I was looking at the butchered remains of a human. I can only think that it was there as a horrific warning, because chained looking at it were three other women, their mouths gagged, hands cuffed and tethered to a metal bar set in the floor.

The room stank of shit, blood, and guts, and I had no desire to stay any longer. With my strength behind the blows the machete broke the thin chains, and the girls were on their feet. I left them gagged, though; I knew the screams would be coming.

"This way!" I said in Spanish. "This way! Follow me!"

Like terrified sheep they followed me up the stairs. I was on the final step when all of the lights went out, the noise from the TV died, and I heard sirens in the near distance.

"Fuck."

CHAPTER 40

The bad guy cavalry was coming, and I needed more weapons. I needed more time.

"Hold this." I said to one of the girls, and gave her a thin flashlight from my pocket. By that light I went to work on the cuffs, and quickly had them out of them. "Follow me." I told them again, leading them to the window that I'd taken out. My plan had been to drive the girls to safety, but now that the police sirens were on the street, that was out of the question. We were out of time, and I'd need to cause a distraction as they figured out the rest themselves. I didn't even have a second to enjoy the irony that the police arriving here was possibly the worst thing that could happen for the girls' survival chances, and my own. Either way, the course for them was to run.

They didn't hug me. Didn't thank me. That's some movie bullshit. They were too terrified for any of that. They were acting on instinct, pure and simple, and they bolted like a farm animal with the gate left open.

Checking my pistol, I moved toward the front door, checking myself as I saw it was already open. That pause saved my life as a bat came swinging out of the dark, missing me by inches. I fired two shots into the darkness, got rewarded with a scream, and got six more shots back at me.

All detail was lost at that point. I've been involved in close quarter battle more times than I can count, but never like this. I don't know how many of them there were, how many I killed, who was police, and who were cartel. I just know that I fired the pistol until it was empty, hacked with my machete until it broke, and stabbed with the kitchen knife until it got stuck in somebody's chest. I had blood in my eyes, my mouth, my nose, my ears. I could taste my enemy. Smell them. I probably pissed myself. I definitely tasted puke. I had to get out. I had to run, and in the darkness I tried to fight my way back to a window. Any window.

But something hit me hard across my leg, and I went down.

CHAPTER 41

I didn't have time to worry about what put me down, I just knew I had to get back up. There were voices screaming and shouting in Spanish, and by the washing light of the police cars I saw a boot flying in towards my face. With my switchblade in my hand I swung out to protect myself, and felt the metal cut into leather. The boot pulled back, coming in for another try, but then there were gunshots, and a scream.

"Stop shooting!" Someone shouted. "You hit Sebastian!"

Friendly fire. It happens to bad guys too. This was my chance. Probably my last. I took it, and charged for the window. There was no stopping me, and I came on like Aaron Donald, feeling my shoulder smash into god knows who…

And then I was out of the window.

CHAPTER 42

I threw my jacket onto the glass on the wall but it still tore into me as I pulled myself up and over, and I felt blood running from my hands and legs. My heart was beating out of my mouth and my lungs were hanging out of my ass, but I ran like a fucking Olympian for the Camry. I expected a chase, but the cops were either looking the other way, or in the house, and so I forced myself to be calm, and to pull away from the curb like I was heading to the store to pick up a paper. My eyes worked overtime on my mirrors, but after two minutes of driving my pulse began to slow, and I could finally breathe again; I'd made it.

Now I just had to make it home.

CHAPTER 43

Do you know what's not fun? Washing blood off of you in a dirty ass little river in Juarez, but what choice did I have? I used a bridge for cover, and went to work under that thing like a fucking troll. I had a basic med kit with me in the Camry, and I used butterfly stitches to close up my cuts as best as I could. Lucky for me desert nights were cold, and so I'd be able to wear gloves to cover the wounds on my hands as I crossed back into America. My face was another matter. A ball cap would give me shadow, but I knew I'd taken a beating. I put makeup on the bruises, but I'm no Kim Kardashian, and I washed it off when I saw I looked more like someone from the Adams family. I dumped my bloody kit in the water, and in fresh clothes, struck out for home.

CHAPTER 44

If you ever want to cross a border after committing a crime, try and do it at the busiest time of day. Luckily for me, four AM in Juarez was one of those times, as migrant workers began their daily crossing into The States. With my American plates and passport, I hardly even got a second look.

I dropped the Camry at the rental place and then walked to my truck. It gave me ten minutes to finally think of something more than immediate survival, and I could look back on the night.

I knew that I was lucky to be alive. I had no right to walk out of that place alive. I took my switchblade out of my pocket, and thought about the boot that had been coming for my face. If that had connected, I'd probably be getting skinned alive right now.

Instead I picked up my truck, and after putting in some anti-tail maneuvers through El Paso, headed to my ranch.

I surprised myself that I was disappointed when I realized that Diego wasn't there. The house felt kinda empty as I took a beer from the fridge, and warmed up some food. The microwave hadn't even pinged before I'd fallen asleep at the kitchen table. I must have been there for eight hours before I finally came to, feeling about as bad as I ever had done in my life. I thought back to the cartel guy I'd hit with the truck; I guess I knew how he felt.

I was about to drift off again when my phone began to vibrate. I looked at it, and saw two missed calls; they were from Anna-Maria.

"Hello?"

The voice on the far end sounded almost as worn out as I felt. "What do you have going on tonight?" She asked me, straight off the bat. "I need a drink."

I sat back in my chair. Every muscle ached. Every bone throbbed. "You know what?" I grunted. "I think I do, too."

CHAPTER 45

When I get to the bar Anna-Maria is waiting for me, and so is a cold beer.

"How are you doing?" I ask her. She looks almost as tired as I feel.

"I hate this border." She tells me honestly. "It's selfish of me, but I just feel like going away for a while."

"So do it." I shrug, but she shakes her head.

"There's people dying down here everyday. Shit, I don't need to tell you how it is, Dom." She says gently.

That's probably why I'm here, I realize. She wants someone who can talk about the border without actually needing to talk about it. Just someone who *knows*. It's the same reason that so many war veterans hang out together. Doesn't mean you talk about it all the time, but everyone *knows.*

I stand up. "Let me get us another beer."

I get the feeling that it's going to be a long night, and honestly, my body's feeling a little less beat up after the first. Anna-Maria's eyes don't hurt either. There's still something behind them that lures me. That spark of danger.

"You don't strike me as your usual charity type." I tell her honestly. "You got a bit more… edge."

She smiles. It's a good smile. "And how many charity workers you met, Dom?"

Shit. She's got me with that one. "I guess I'm stereotyping, huh?"

That smile again. She doesn't hold it against me.

"Hey, let me get dinner tonight, make that one up to you."

Anna-Maria looks at the drink in her hand. "We could do that," she says, placing the bottle down. "Or, you could take me home and fuck me?"

CHAPTER 46

We didn't make it home, at least not at first. It started in the parking lot, and we'd just about cleared the limits of town when Anna-Maria told me to pull the truck down a dirt road. We just about made it home for the second round, and I lost count after that. I've had women before that felt like they were trying to fuck their demons away - who the fuck would come to me if they had their life together? - but Anna-Maria was something else. By the time that we finally stopped to sleep, I felt like the cartel guys at the house had beat the shit out of me for a second time.

A few hours later, dawn begins to spill in through the open window. We're both naked on top of the sheets, her arm across me but face in the pillow. I hope she doesn't wake up, not yet. Not because I don't want her to, but because I *do* want her to. This is not the time to be catching feelings for someone. Shit is complicated enough as it is, and I still need to get my hands on that motherfucker Lopez.

Maybe she feels my tension, because she suddenly comes to, like she was having a bad dream.

"Are you okay?" I ask her quickly.

She sees me, and the moment of panic drops away. She looks calm. Maybe I've deluded myself, but it's like she feels… protected.

I want to ask her what happened in her life to make her wake up like that, and that's as sure a sign as any that this woman is under my skin, now.

"Hey." I say. "Can I make you some breakfast?"

She smiles, and moves her hand to my chest, but then… "Jesus, Dom, how'd you get all these bruises?"

I prop myself up, and look down at my body; Fuck. I look like a piñata that had a really hard day at the office, but you don't last as an NCO if you can't scramble bullshit quickly: "I came off my goddamn dirt bike." I tell her, doing my best to sound like an embarrassed idiot. It must work, because the next second she starts kissing me at my shoulders, and she doesn't stop.

When we're done, I insist that she relax and I walk to the kitchen to bring us breakfast in bed. I know I'm playing house. I know it won't last. But you know what? Fuck it. I *want* to play house with this woman. She gives a fuck about people. She gives a fuck about *me.*

"Do your thing, Dom." I have to say to myself, like I'm a third person. It's so rare in my life that I think this way that it almost does feel like there is a different person in the room.

I'm battered and bruised but I'm feeling pretty proud that someone like Anna-Maria would be interested in me, and so I'm trying not to move like an old man as I put the eggs on the stove, and start mixing pancakes. Once everything's rolling, I look around the kitchen; our clothes are everywhere. We didn't make it to the bedroom before they came off.

I feel a hundred years old as I bend down to pick up and fold the clothes, and finally I get to the first things to come off; our boots.

I'm setting them next to each other, loving every second of happy families, when I see the groove of a knife's blade cut into the front of her boot.

CHAPTER 47

The first thing I feel when I see the cut in Anna-Maria's boot is acid in my stomach, and panic. The next thing is embarrassment, and I call myself an idiot. There are so many ways to fuck up a boot. What I'm thinking is just stupid. It's impossible.

But my stomach is churning. There's one easy way to know for sure if Anna-Maria's boot was the one that tried to kick me in the safe house.

I keep the boot in my hands and step over to my pile of clothes. I reach inside the pocket of my jeans, and take out my switchblade.

I click it open, and pause. It's like I already know, and I can feel a tide rising in my throat. I've never wanted to be wrong so much in my life.

But then I move the blade to the boot, and I know that I'm not.

It's a perfect fit.

CHAPTER 48

I smell food burning. It snaps me from me trance. I look one more time at my switchblade sitting snugly in the groove it had cut into Anna-Maria's boot.

I put her boot down, but keep the blade in my hand. What the fuck do I do now? I know there has to be a rational explanation for this, but how do I find it?

By making breakfast. I tell myself. Make breakfast. Maintain. Pretend that everything's still perfect. The answers will come.

I take a deep breath. Her voice comes from the bedroom. "Everything okay in there, Dom? I smell burning."

Suck it up. Maintain. Get your answers. "All good. I just suck at cooking, that's all."

"Want some help?"

"Nah, I got it. On my way."

I leave my switchblade open beneath my pile of clothes, and then I shovel the burnt food onto a couple of plates. Finally I pour coffee. I watch the steam rise before I put everything onto a tray, and carry it into the bedroom.

"Hey, babe."

CHAPTER 49

I deserve a fucking Oscar for the way I pushed my acid back into my stomach and ate that food with a smile on my face. Benefits of having the shit kicked out of you by your parents and classmates, I guess. You get good at hiding the hurt.

"That was good." She smiles at me, and I feel sick. "What do you wanna do now?"

There's an invitation in her words, but I've got my own. "Let's take a walk. It's beautiful out right now."

That's no lie. The sun close to dawn is like a hug from a friend, not the punch in the face it becomes later in the day.

"Sounds good. Do you remember where my clothes are?"

Yeah, I fucking remember. "This way."

I offer her a hand so that I can make sure I'm behind her as I playfully steer her towards the kitchen. I pull my boxers and jeans on first, then my boots. She starts top down. My switchblade is a few inches from my hand, hidden beneath my t-shirt. She begins to tie her laces. It's time to ask.

"What happened to your boot?"

She doesn't skip a beat. She leans forward to inspect it. "Huh. No idea."

I shouldn't push it, but I do. I was a grunt, not a spook; "Seems like something you'd remember. Looks deep."

Anna-Maria just keeps on lacing. "Oh, no, these aren't mine. I got my boots soaked yesterday down at the river, so I borrowed these from one of the girls on my team."

Relief floods through me and I want to punch the air like I just won the goddamn Super Bowl. I'm so happy that I almost forget there was a reason behind my worry. These boots belong to someone, and they tried to stomp my face.

"Hey," I say, and the change in my tone makes Anna-Maria stop what she's doing, and sit back to look at me.

"What is it, Dom?"

I take a breath. "Do you trust me?" I ask.

"If I didn't would I be out here?" There's an edge of confusion in her words, but they convince me.

"Well I need you to trust me now, okay?" She nods. "Those boots." I say. "Who do they belong to?"

Her confusion grows, but she answers. "A girl on my team." Anna-Maria tells me. "Silvia Lopez."

CHAPTER 50

I say nothing but I can feel my skin prickle. Silvia *Lopez*. Jesus fucking Christ. The leader of the kidnappers is in Anna-Maria's charity. It makes so much sense. Where better to find vulnerable illegals to kidnap than from a charity that's set up to help them?

"Dom…" Anna-Maria says, reading me, "is there something I need to be worried about?"

I don't know what to say.

"Has Silvia done… Dom, what's going on?"

I go down to one knee so that my eyes are the same level as hers. I place my hand on her shoulder, and look straight into her eyes; for the first time, I see fear in them.

"I've got you, okay?"

"Got me from what, Dom?"

I shake my head. "I can't tell you everything right now." But I will. I know I will. I trust this woman. "I know it's asking a lot, but I need you to do something for me?"

She hesitates, but I don't blame her. I'm asking her to put blind faith in me. "Anna-Maria, you came to me because you trusted me to do the right thing. Please. Trust me now."

She slowly nods. "What do you need, Dom?"

I smile sadly. What's coming next won't be easy for any of us.

"I need you to introduce me to Silvia Lopez."

CHAPTER 51

Anna-Maria wanted to ask me questions - lots of questions - but she must have seen in my eyes that she wouldn't get answers.

"Just trust me." I promised her.

The truck cab was quiet as I drove her back to the bar to collect her own. I kissed her, and her arms went around my neck. There was no passion, there. Just worry.

"You don't have to do this if you don't want to." I told her.

I felt her shake her head, her words into my shoulder. "I'll do it. I trust you."

Alone I drove to the office. Usually, this was my sanctuary. A place where my mind was lost on other people's problems, not my own, but the ice-cold fingers of dread were clawing at my stomach, their touch growing stronger and stronger; was Silvia Lopez *the* Lopez? A family member? Someone else in the kidnap gang who happened to share the same name? Would they get spooked? Would they hurt Anna-Maria? Would they kidnap her? Would they torture her?

I tried to calm my mind. Silvia Lopez was Anna-Maria's teammate. There was no reason she wouldn't trust her. No reason she'd see the request to go with Anna-Maria as anything other than just another day at the office.

"Hey Dom, you okay?" It was Ortega. He handed me a coffee. "You look like shit."

"Thanks," I said, sipping the caffeine. "Came off my bike."

He half-smiled. "Mind on other things, huh?"

I nodded, and the older guy looked at me for a second. It was the kind of look an NCO gives to his junior guys. A little worry. A little pride.

"Nothing better than the love of a good woman," he told me, and I knew there was more coming, "and nothing better at distracting you on the job, either."

"I won't let it affect my work, Orty."

He shook his head. I'd misunderstood him. "Not your work, Dom. You. Border's a dangerous place."

"I got it."

"Good." He grinned. "You're a big mother fucker. I'd lose half the office to lower back injuries if we had to carry your coffin."

He smirked and left.

"Thanks for the coffee."

Ortega was right, I knew. The border was a dangerous place, and I was part of the reason why. Having people that I cared about fucked up the simplicity of violence that I wanted, but what the fuck was I supposed to do about it?

I picked up the coffee in one hand and my phone in the other, and walked out into the heat of the parking lot.

"Hey Sarah," I said as she answered. "How are things going with Diego?"

"We're having a good time." She told me. "I'm learning a lot about superheroes."

I smiled at that.

"Hey, Dom." She said quietly, and from the change in her voice's echo, I figured that she'd stepped into the bathroom. "I need to go to the funeral directors today. Is he okay to be on his own, because…"

Because otherwise he'll figure out that it's his mom and Ethan going into the dirt.

"He'll be fine." I said. "He's a good kid."

And he deserves to know the truth, I thought to myself. As soon as Lopez is dealt with, I'll tell him.

We said our goodbyes and I turned back to the office.

I'd only taken a step when my phone vibrated. It was a text from Anna-Maria.

Your ranch, 6PM.

I'll have company.

CHAPTER 52

It said everything you need to know about Juarez that the news of the killings in the safe house hadn't even reached my office. There was a little talk about the tunnel house, but most of the agents had even moved on from that; there were just too many bodies, warm and cold, that needed dealing with. You didn't get a chance to draw your breath - the border saw to that.

Ortega must have sensed I was off because he kept me in the building working on papers. Most days I'd have pushed against that, but today it suited me just fine. I finished my shift and started the drive back to the ranch, turning my mind over to what would happen at eighteen hundred; Anna-Maria was coming with Silvia Lopez, and whether or not she was *the* Lopez, the mother fucker had tried to kill me, and she was part of the kidnap crew. How was I going to deal with her? Could I just ask Anna-Maria to walk away? Was I willing to kill a defenseless woman?

I thought a long time about that last question. It was the thought of the torture that Lucia had suffered that sealed it. Yes, defenseless woman or not, I would kill her if she was the one responsible.

I'd promised Ethan that I'd kill them all, and I would not break that oath to my brother.

I parked in front of my house, checked that I had a round chambered in my pistol, and put it into the small of my back. I had my switchblade in my pocket, and I put another into my boot. I didn't know which it would be, but I did know that one of those tools was about to even a score.

I looked at my watch; six o' clock. Almost on the dot, I heard the sound of a truck in the distance.

Time to meet Lopez.

CHAPTER 53

Anna-Maria's truck pulled to a stop. She looked nervous.

She was alone.

I stepped forward as she opened her door. "Are you okay? Where is she?"

She hugged me and kissed me. The kind of kiss you give someone when you're worried about them.

"I dropped her a little further south." She told me. "I don't know what this is about Dom, and I trust you, but whatever it is, it doesn't seem like a good idea that she should know where you live…"

Her eyes asked me if she was right. I nodded. "Thank you."

Anna-Maria pushed a strand of blonde hair from her face and gave me a nervous smile. "I told her that we're meeting a group of illegals that are crossing."

"How far from here?"

"A ten minute walk."

"Do you think she suspects something's up"

She shook her head. "We do this kind of thing a lot."

I pulled her close. "Thank you for doing this."

Anna-Maria smiled weakly, and I hated

myself for bringing her into this shit storm.

"Let's go." I said. "Let's get this over with."

We didn't speak as we walked. The brush was thickening; perfect cover for illegals, and I wondered how many crossed my land that I had no idea about. I thought about asking Anna-Maria, but now wasn't the time.

I looked at her out of the corner of my eye. She looked nervous, and I couldn't blame her; you could smell violence in the air.

"How far?" I asked quietly.

"She's waiting in those trees." She said, and I felt overcome with the need to protect her. "Walk behind me." I told her. "It'll be okay, I promise."

She swallowed, and fell in behind me as I walked quietly to the thick stand of trees. The sun was high, casting shadow beneath me, and I was nearly on top of it before I saw the shine of metal against the dirt.

I took another step, and saw that there was no woman waiting for me here...

Only a shovel.

I turned, and saw the gun in Anna-Maria's hand.

"*Lopez.*"

CHAPTER 54

I didn't know whether to puke or cry when I saw the pistol aimed at my chest. My life had been one long series of betrayals; why had I expected this time to be any different?

I want to cuss at her. Charge at her. But the gun in her hand is a .45, and it'll take a hole out of me before I can get my hands on her. I don't want to die. At least not until I fulfill my promise to Ethan.

And so I say nothing. If this bitch wants me to dig my own grave, I'll not make it easy. I'll wait for a chance.

"Keep your hands straight up." She tells me, no wobble in her voice. "Now turn around." Comes the next order, and once again my back's to her. "Use your left hand to slowly take out your pistol, finger and thumb. You move fast, I'll put a hole in the bottom of your spine, and leave you out here for the coyotes."

I have no doubt that she means it. I take the pistol out as she tells me, and toss it out of the stand of trees.

"Now slowly, walk to the shovel. Slower than that!"

She keeps the perfect distance behind

me. I'm not close enough to make a grab, not far enough to run. She's a clever bitch, and even the shovel is a short handled kind to make it useless to me right now. Useless except for digging my grave, that is.

Anna-Maria - *Lopez* - keeps the pistol in both hands, but close to her chest. I'm a big guy and she can't miss me even before she punches out to be fully drawn down. "You know what to do."

I start digging. As the metal cuts into the dirt, I hear the words fall out of my mouth. "I'm digging this for you, you fucking cunt."

There's no laugh from her. No smile. She looks more worn out than ever, those dangerous eyes in a face that's showing lines before its time. "Don't make this any harder than it needs to be, Dom."

Well, I've heard that one before, but this isn't the kind of breakup I'm used to, no matter how bad things got. "You're fucking evil." I can't help myself saying. "Exploiting the people you pretend to help? There's a special place in hell for you. A special fucking place."

It's then that her expression changes, and she looks at me like a child. "*Exploiting?*" She sneers. "How fucking dumb are you, Dom? I thought you were more than just a Grunt, but can you really not see past the end of your dick?"

I don't know what she's talking about, but fuck it. I drive the shovel into the dirt, and turn my eyes fully onto her. At the bar she felt the need to unload her shit. Maybe she'll do it again. I'd like to know why I'm about to die.

From my look she breaks, willingly. It's as if she's scolding a child with shitty grades. "You ever make an omelette, Dom?"

It's not enough for her to kill me. Now the bitch is attacking my cooking.

"The border is *fucked,* Dom." She curses. "You know this! Every year, thousands of people are dying, and *nobody cares.*

"Ten years I've been down here, and I can't even say that there's been one single week where I thought things were getting better! There's no hope! There's just misery."

"Misery that you cause!" I shouted, wanting to plow the spade into her head. "You killed my friend, you fucking bitch! You tortured her! And I'll fucking kill you for it!"

My threat goes straight over her head. Why wouldn't it when she was the one holding the gun, and I was on my knees.

"You think I *enjoy* that, Dom?" She asks, a crack in her voice. "You think

I enjoy it? How much sleep do you think I'm getting, huh? You think I saw my life turning out this way?"

She shakes her head, then emphasizes every word. "I. Do. What. I. Do. For. The. Greater. Good.

"No one cares about extortion down here! Fuck, no one even cares about bodies anymore! That's why it had to be Lucia and all of the others!"

The reason behind Lucia's death hits me like a brick, and I think back to Sarah's files on the kidnap victims, so many of them with next of kin in the military…

"You're trying to start a war." I realize.

She nods savagely. "It's the only kind of message our country understands!

"No one in the rest of America wants to look down, Dom. They don't want to *see!* The only way to change that is to start a war."

And what better way to do it than to provoke soldiers into taking on the war in a way that no agency can? I'd walked straight into the trap that she'd baited with her collateral damage. Ethan had been her target, but she'd gotten a Ranger on the loose all the same.

"I'm sorry, okay Dom? I'm sorry." And maybe she was, but she'd killed and tortured my friend. There was no path to redemption for her.

I started to turn back to the shovel, but she shook her head.

"Enough is enough." She punched out the pistol. "Close your eyes."

CHAPTER 55

"Close your eyes!" She snapped.

I didn't. I wasn't about to make this easier for her. I kept my eyes open and staring hard into hers. I knew what she'd done to Lucia and many others, but had she ever killed someone she'd shared intimacy with? I was certain that she hadn't known I was behind the safe house until I asked her about the boot, and Lopez. Fuck it.

"Did you ever actually give a shit?"

I saw her swallow. "Just close your eyes."

I wouldn't. Her knuckles were bright white on the pistol grip.

"Close your eyes, Dom."

I wouldn't.

"CLOSE YOUR FUCKING EYES!"

No.

And then, a gunshot.

CHAPTER 56

The sound of a shot crashed through the trees; not the boom of a .45, but the crack of a 9mm that clipped Anna-Maria's backpack, sending her spinning on her axis. I didn't wait to figure out who, or how. I just charged.

She saw me coming, and pulled the .45's trigger on instinct, but she was shocked and not aiming, and only got off two wild shots before I was on her, putting my weight on top of her, and driving my skull down into her face. I felt her nose collapse, blood run into my eyes, and I did it again and again as I held onto her wrists. I felt the moment she gave up her grip on her pistol, and by the time that I'd backed up onto my knees, she was unrecognizable, and no threat to me.

But she was alive, and I didn't want that.

I stood up and grabbed the .45. Aimed it at her face. I didn't know where the first shot had come from, and I didn't care. If it were law enforcement, I was willing to go to prison to see out my oath to my brother.

I looked down at my woman at my feet. She had taken from me everything that I loved. I just had to move my finger a few millimeters, and Lopez would be gone from the world.

Then I heard a sound to my left.

"Uncle Dominic…"

Diego stepped into the clearing.

CHAPTER 57

The kid was visibly trembling as he took in the sight in front of him; his uncle stood over a woman with a smashed face. Walking up on this he had the right to be terrified of me, but when I saw what was in his hand, I knew Diego was a witness to the truth.

He was holding my gun.

He saw my eyes, and took on the look of a kid who knows that he's in trouble. "My Dad, he… he… he told me to never shoot unless he was around. I'm sorry, Uncle Dominic."

His Dad. *Ethan.* I lowered my own pistol then. Diego didn't need to see this.

"Its okay." I told him. "You saved my life." And I knew that deep down in my soul, my brother had saved it too. Because of love he'd taught Diego how to shoot, and I had no doubt that he was the reason I was still drawing breath.

I look down at Anna-Maria. I want her dead, but I can't help but hear the words of the Ranger Creed. Words that Ethan and I had shouted out shoulder to shoulder as we stood on parade grounds and chest deep in swamps; "I will always endeavor to uphold the prestige, honor, and high esprit de corps of The Rangers."

Where was the honor in killing a defenseless person?

Thinking of those words, and looking at Diego, I knew what Ethan would want to change in his last moments; "look after the kid." That's what he'd want.

"Come here."

Diego ran to me and I pulled him in tight with my free arm. "How the hell did you find me?" I ask him.

He looked sheepish, but I encouraged him to be honest. "You saved my life." I said again.

He told me everything, the poor kid. When Sarah had gone out, Diego had been flipping through channels when he came across the news, and saw a story about a local veteran who'd died after his girlfriend had "drowned" in the river.

Guilt boiled up from my stomach. "I'm sorry. You shouldn't have found out that way. I should have told you."

The kid said nothing. His eyes were being drawn to the woman on the ground.

"Is that…." He was a smart boy.

"Yes."

"Are you going to kill her?" There was fear in the voice.

I shook my head. "Criminals go to prison."

I saw relief flood his features.

There'd been enough death.

"I want to go home, Uncle Dominic."

And so I picked up the criminal, and then we went home.

EPILOGUE

One week later.

Rows of trees, a flag in the breeze, and two headstones side by side. This is where my brother and Lucia were laid to rest. This is where I, and their son, will visit them until our own time has passed.

Diego is beside me, pressed shirt tucked into his pants, and childlike confusion on his face. He knows that his mother and Ethan are gone, but he still doesn't know what that means.

To the other side of him is Sarah. There are tears on her cheeks, and her hand holds Diego's. She's taking him back to Dallas. I offered her the money I'd taken from the tunnel house, but she wants to do things properly. Until I have a use for it, that cash will stay buried.

It's Sarah who took Anna-Maria into custody. The FBI were eager to get their hands on the person known as Lopez. I was worried that sparing her life meant my own actions would become clear, but my mind was put to rest after Sarah had visited me with a man with no name. If my sins were known, they were forgiven, at least in their eyes.

Diego lets go of Sarah's hand, and takes something from his pocket before placing it on Ethan's headstone. It's a Sugarman mask, the kid is convinced that Ethan's spirit is the superhero the border needs. The stories have been spreading. Three kidnap victims made it out alive to tell anyone who'd listen about the person that had saved them. A lone wolf. A vigilante.

The Sugarman.

Sarah meets my look, and with a smile, she leads Diego back to the waiting truck and its new windows. As he walks away, I hear Diego singing the folk song that has crossed the border with the illegals, and spread through El Paso. I could hear some of the soft words he was singing...

El cielo me bendijo,
los rayos del sol me cobijan.
Ah llegado una esperanza,
aquel que cuida de nuestras vidas.

Nos protegé de los males,
nuestros pasos El mantiene,
dia y noche El nos vela,
a vengado a los carteles.

Chorus

Nuestros muertos an mandado,
a un espiritu nocturno,

a El que le llamamos Santo,
como El no ay ninguno.

Si un mal se nos acerca,
de pronto cai como sin vida,
Mi Santo 'El Sugarman'
a ti rezo por mi vida.

His words fade away. I look from Lucia's headstone, to my brother's. I look at the Sugarman mask. Think of the people who are singing his song.

Maybe violence isn't the answer on the border, but it's the only one I've got. Should I close my eyes? Turn my back?

Four letters make up my mind. Four letters that shaped my life. They look back at the from Ethan's headstone like a commandment.

R. L. T. W.

Rangers Lead The Way.

All the fucking way.

I reach out, and pick up the mask.

The End

Corrido of The Sugarman

'El Sugarman'
By:Humberto Gloria

El cielo me bendijo,
los rayos del sol me cobijan.
Ah llegado una esperanza,
aquel que cuida de nuestras vidas.

Nos protegé de los males,
nuestros pasos El mantiene,
dia y noche El nos vela,
a vengado a los carteles.

Chorus

Nuestros muertos an mandado,
a un espiritu nocturno,
a El que le llamamos Santo,
como El no ay ninguno.

Si un mal se nos acerca,
de pronto cai como sin vida,
Mi Santo 'El Sugarman'
a ti rezo por mi vida.

'My Saint- El Sugarman' - English Translation

By: Humberto Gloria

The heavens have blessed me,
the suns rays blanket me,
a hope has arrived,
he who is the protector of our lives.

He watches over us from the evils,
he sustains our path,
day and night he is our watch-keeper
he has avenged us from Cartels.

Chorus

Our dead have sent a Saint,
a nocturnal spirit,
he whom we call Saint,
like him there is no other.

If evil approaches us,
swiftly they fall lifeless,
My Saint The Sugarman
to you I pray to keep my life.

Acknowledgment

Thanks to Tom Marcus and Jason Piccolo for introducing us to each other, and setting the ball rolling on this series. We're grateful to Ernest at OAF Nation for allowing us to use the skull design, and to Luke Romyn and Rich for their work on the cover.

Thanks to Kendra Middleton Williams for some great suggestions and catches in the editing.

Final thanks go to the Border Patrol. In particular, Del Rio Sector, Eagle Pass North, Bravo Unit. E3755555555. Dirty Birds, BORTAC and BORSTAR; *Honor First.*

- Vincent & Geraintv

Printed in Great Britain
by Amazon